THE PURPLE PLAGUE

The first victim was a shopkeeper in Bradford. A week later, a publican in Newcastle had collapsed into a coma and later died. Inexorably, similar deaths followed, all in different parts of the country. It appeared that a new form of bacillus was involved. Where had it originated from, how had it arrived into the country, and why did it occur in such diverse places? Dubbed by the press as the 'Purple Plague', was the disease natural? *Or man-made. . . ?*

DERWENT STEELE

THE PURPLE PLAGUE

Complete and Unabridged

LINFORD
Leicester

First published in Great Britain

First Linford Edition
published 2013

A catalogue record for this book is available
from the British Library.

ISBN 978–1–4448–1655–6

Published by
F. A. Thorpe (Publishing)
Anstey, Leicestershire

Set by Words & Graphics Ltd.
Anstey, Leicestershire
Printed and bound in Great Britain by
T. J. International Ltd., Padstow, Cornwall

This book is printed on acid-free paper

1

The Murder at Staines

John Blackmore had just finished his breakfast and having poured himself out a third cup of coffee and lit a cigarette, was engaged in leisurely running through the pile of correspondence that had arrived by that morning's post. As was his wont he pencilled notes on the margin of each as he scanned their contents before laying them aside for Cartwright, his secretary, to answer later.

The morning was clear and bright with that sharp, unmistakable tang that betokens Autumn, in the fresh crisp air and outside, in Mecklinburg Square a flood of sunshine had successfully fought and vanquished the mists of the previous night.

Harry Cartwright, seated opposite his employer, was dividing his attention between his plate and the newspaper, which he had propped up against the milk jug in front of him. He had reached for his cup and was in the act of raising it to his lips when he paused suddenly, with it held in mid-air half way between the saucer and his mouth. His attention had been attracted to an item of news, the splashed headlines of which covered two columns: 'Another Victim of the Purple Plague. Well known banker dies of mysterious disease!'

He set his cup down, its contents un-tasted.

'There's been another mysterious death, Mr. Blackmore!' he remarked. 'In London this time, and as before, the doctors are completely baffled. This makes the fourth in the last two months. You know it's getting serious. I wonder what can be the cause of it?'

Blackmore raised his eyes from the letter he had been reading and regarded his secretary with a little gleam of interest.

'The theory held by the medical profession,' he replied, 'is that some new and hitherto unknown disease has made its appearance in this country from abroad. The theory is quite a possible one, though in my opinion there are one or two points against it, one, in particular, being the fact that up to the present no two deaths have occurred in the same locality. The characteristics in this new case are the same as those in the others, I suppose?'

Cartwright nodded, his mouth full of toast.

'According to the paper, exactly the same,' he answered when he was able to speak.

'Let me have a look at the account,' said John, pushing aside the pile of letters at the side of his plate. 'I'm rather interested.'

Harry handed him the paper and below the sprawling headlines Blackmore read the report:

'Mr. Gordon Wilberthorne, the Managing Director of the South Eastern and Scottish Bank, is the latest victim to succumb to the unknown malady, the Purple Plague, which has recently made its appearance in various parts of the country, and has already caused considerable controversy among the Medical Profession. Yesterday morning Mr. Wilberthorne attended a meeting of the Board of Director's at the Bank's premises in Lombard Street. Towards the end of this meeting he complained of feeling indisposed, but insisted on carrying on the business on which he was engaged. When the meeting was over, however, he stated that he was feeling considerably worse and decided to suspend all further business for the day and go home. He drove to his residence in Grosvenor Square and arriving there went straight to his study, giving orders that he was going to rest and was not to be disturbed till teatime. At four-thirty the butler tapped on the door of the study with the intention of asking whether his master would like tea served in that room. Getting no reply to his repeated knocking he entered and found Mr. Wilberthorne unconscious in his chair before the fire. The butler thought at first that he was sleeping and tried to arouse him, but without success. Feeling alarmed he telephoned for the doctor. Dr. Lingard, who lived but a few doors away, hurried round immediately and made every effort to bring Mr. Wilberthorne back to consciousness, but without avail.

'Considerably puzzled as to the nature of the illness from which the banker was suffering the doctor called in Sir Lionel Trencham, the well-known specialist. They held a hurried consultation and did everything in their power, but in spite of their efforts, shortly after nine o'clock Mr. Wilberthorne died without recovering from the state of coma in which he had remained since he had been first found by the butler.

'Sir Lionel states that there can be no doubt that his death was due to the mysterious malady that has made its appearance in this country during the last two months and which has already accounted for three fatalities, in the Midlands, the North of England and Scotland. The symptoms in Mr. Wilberthorne's case are precisely the same as in the other two victims; the strange coma, accompanied by stertorous breathing, the

5

peculiar mauve-like rash, which as usual appeared immediately after death and spread all over the body, from the head to the feet were present, unmistakable characteristics of this new and terrible pestilence. As in the other cases also, the fingers and toes of the dead man quickly became bloodless and white, and as brittle as glass so that on the slightest touch they were liable to break off, a condition in some respects similar to frostbite.

'Mr. Gordon Wilberthorne makes the fourth victim of the 'Purple Plague' and the medical profession appears to be helpless to deal with the disease, since at the present time they are completely ignorant of its origin. It can only be hoped that something can be done at the earliest possible moment to discover a means of fighting this dreadful menace, for should it become prevalent and an epidemic break out, the imagination can scarcely cope with the picture of the horrors that would result.'

There was half a column more on the same lines, followed by an article in which a leading specialist expressed his views concerning the origin of the disease.

Although John Blackmore read it carefully there was nothing that was likely to lead to or even suggest a cure.

The 'Purple Plague', a name that had been given to the disease by an enterprising journalist, had first made its appearance about two months previously, the victim being the owner of a small tobacconist's shop in Bradford. A week later another death occurred in Newcastle. This time it had been a publican who had been attacked by the strange malady. He had been taken ill during a visit to a theatre and had gradually got worse. Half way through the evening, his wife, who had accompanied him, insisted on his going home. He had scarcely arrived there when he collapsed into a state of coma and later died, in spite of the attention of the doctors who had been hastily summoned to his aid.

Blackmore had been considerably interested at the time, but although he had spent an appreciable amount of time in trying to evolve some theory to account for the sudden appearance of the malady and its possible origin, he had been forced in the end to confess himself beaten. The symptoms had no parallel in medical science, nothing to give the doctors a starting point on which to commence their investigations. Blood tests had been made from the body fluid taken from the victims after death and under the microscope these had revealed traces of baccilli, but in such an entirely new form that not one of the specialists was able to give them a name or even to suggest a cause for their appearance.

Three weeks elapsed, and then another death occurred, this time in Scotland. A bus conductor in Edinburgh contracted the disease and died exhibiting exactly the same symptoms as in the other two cases. Several specialists journeyed to Scotland especially to conduct the post mortem examination of the body and returned no wiser than when they went. The disease apparently was not contagious for various tests carried out had proved this fact.

To Blackmore the most puzzling part of the whole affair was the fact that the 'Purple Plague' was not confined to any one area. It had appeared first in Bradford, then miles away in Newcastle and thirdly in Scotland; now it had made its appearance in London. To the detective, that was the greatest argument against it being some obscure disease brought over from abroad, in that case it would, without doubt, be more localised. In each of the towns visited by the 'Purple Plague' only one person had been stricken with the pestilence, which suggested the fact that they and they only had come in contact with the object, whatever it was that carried the germ setting up this strange disease.

The newspapers published leading articles about it, each one having a fresh theory to account for its appearance, and for a long time it had been a general topic of conversation everywhere. After the case in Edinburgh nothing else had been heard of the malady, public interest had gradually waned; now this new case had appeared in London to fan the dying flame back to life.

'The most extraordinary thing!' said John, as he laid down the newspaper and blew a cloud of smoke ceiling-wards. 'I must say I'm intensely interested, though I haven't the remotest idea what can be at the bottom of it. The doctors have proved that the disease is caused by a new germ and at present unknown to science, but where it comes from, how it got to the country at all, and why it should appear in places so far distant from one another is a complete mystery.'

'It might be contained in some special kind of food,' suggested Cartwright. 'Perhaps some new tinned stuff.'

His employer nodded thoughtfully.

'That's quite possible,' he agreed, 'but at the same time I think it's hardly probable, for if that is the correct solution it must be some kind of food that was only eaten by the four people who were attacked to account for the disease.'

'Not necessarily,' answered the secretary. 'The germ may only take effect on a person whose bodily health is in just the right state to receive it. I mean,' he added, 'the blood may have to be in a certain condition for the germ to live and thrive, in the same way that a person whose blood is in good condition is less likely to acquire blood poisoning than one whose blood is impure.'

Blackmore nodded.

'I see what you mean,' he replied. 'If the germ of the 'Purple Plague' is contained in some kind of food, then according to your theory, only four people out of the thousands who must have consumed it were in just the right state of health for the germ to become active and take effect.' He shook his head. 'No, I'm afraid the idea is too far fetched.'

'Well, what's your idea?' asked Cartwright.

John shrugged his shoulders.

'I haven't one,' he admitted candidly. 'At the present moment there have not been sufficient cases for any one to build up a hypothesis, there isn't enough data to work on. That's what's flooring the doctors.'

He had risen to his feet when there

came a sudden violent ringing at the front door bell.

'An early visitor, apparently,' he remarked. 'Wonder who it can be and what they want?'

There came the sound of the front door opening and voices in the hall. A few seconds later the maid entered, carrying a card on a salver. Blackmore took it and glanced at the name inscribed on its white surface with a frown.

'Edward Cranston,' he muttered under his breath. 'I seem to have heard the name somewhere, but I can't recollect where. Show him into the study, will you? Say I'll be with him in a moment.'

The maid departed, and Cartwright looked up at his employer.

'I wonder what it's all about,' he said. 'Must have been something jolly urgent to have brought him out at this hour, it isn't half-past-eight yet.'

'We shall soon know,' said Blackmore, as he crossed to the door. 'I'm certain I've heard the name Cranston before. I shall probably remember where when I've seen the owner. Come into the study as soon as you've finished your coffee.'

As he entered the adjoining room, the visitor, who had been standing by the window impatiently tapping a pair of gold-rimmed pince-nez, which hung about his neck on a thin cord of black silk, turned.

He was an elderly man, with iron grey hair which extended at the sides half way down his cheeks in the form of old-fashioned whiskers. Taken in conjunction with his rather stout figure and his florid face these gave him the appearance of a somewhat successful and prosperous farmer. He advanced to meet John with outstretched hand.

'I don't know whether you remember me, Mr. Blackmore,' he greeted in a rather throaty voice, 'but I had the pleasure of meeting you a little over a year ago in connection with a rather eccentric will of a client of mine, Sir John Morely.'

'I remember you perfectly,' said John as he gripped the outstretched hand, and indeed the mist had cleared from his memory directly the visitor turned from the window, for he never forgot a face, and Edward Cranston's was sufficiently out of the ordinary to impress himself on a far less retentive memory than his.

Cranston was a solicitor, the type of old family lawyer that is fast dying out as the younger generation steps into the shoes left behind by older, and perhaps in many cases wiser men.

'I must apologise for calling so early,' continued Cranston, seating himself in the armchair that John wheeled forward, 'but it is really most urgent.'

He drew a large silk handkerchief from his breast pocket, and wiped the perspiration, which in spite of the cold of the morning stood out in little beads upon his forehead.

Now that his face was fully revealed by the light from the windows John could see that he was suffering from extreme agitation. The signs were unmistakable, the hand holding the handkerchief trembled violently, and although nothing but a miracle could have eradicated the habitual redness of his cheeks the lines of worry were plainly visible about his eyes and in the dark pouches that hung beneath.

'I shall be only too happy to do anything to help you,' he said, seating himself in a chair opposite the lawyer. 'What's the trouble?'

'It's murder, Mr. Blackmore,' said Cranston, in a low voice, 'and the whole affair is so extraordinary that directly I heard of it I made up my mind to come and consult you. You have no doubt heard of James Albrey, the shipping millionaire?'

Blackmore had settled himself back in his chair and in reply to the solicitor's question nodded his head.

'Albrey was a great friend of mine,' continued Cranston. 'He was found murdered this morning in his house at Staines, and — '

'Perhaps it would be as well,' interrupted Blackmore, 'if you would tell me the story from the beginning, I shall then be able to get a better idea of the circumstances.'

The lawyer played nervously with his glasses for a moment, obviously making a great effort to master his emotions before he began.

'As I said just now, Mr. Blackmore,

James Albrey and I were friends, a friendship which dated from our school days and continued ever since. As well as being his friend I was also his legal advisor, and most of his business passed through my hands. Last night, just as I was on the point of retiring I received a telephone message from Wilby, poor Albrey's butler, asking me to come at once to Staines as something dreadful had happened and his master had been murdered. You can imagine the shock with which I received the news and I immediately hurried to Elm Lodge as fast as I could.

'Wilby was waiting to receive me in the hall, and he told me brokenly what had happened. It appears that Albrey, who was a bachelor, dined alone at seven o'clock as usual and then retired to his study, as was his invariable custom. Shortly afterwards a stranger called to see him, giving no name but sending in a note. Albrey read the note and gave orders for the man to be shown into him at once. The interview lasted about twenty minutes and Wilby says that on passing the door of the study on his way from the dining room to the kitchen he heard the sound of voices raised in high altercation. Five minutes after the stranger took his departure, letting himself out.

'After he had gone Wilby entered the study with some coffee. His master was seated in his usual place behind the desk, and appeared to be considerably agitated, and then he informed the butler that he was expecting a lady, who was to be shown in to him immediately on her arrival.'

The lawyer paused for a moment and passed his tongue over his dry lips.

'I trust, Mr. Blackmore,' he said, 'that you will not consider all this superfluous, but I am trying to omit nothing that is likely to have any bearing on what followed.'

'Quite right, Mr. Cranston,' said Blackmore. 'Go on.'

'At eleven o'clock, the lady whom Albrey had been expecting, arrived, accompanied by a young man. Wilby, according to his master's instructions, conducted them to the study and tapped on the door, preparatory to announcing them. Receiving no reply and believing that his master had not heard him, he knocked louder and as there was still no answer, opened the door. It was then he made the terrible discovery. Albrey was still seated behind his desk but he had fallen forward, his head lying on the blotting pad, and protruding from between his shoulder blades was the handle of a knife. He had been stabbed in the back and was stone dead. Wilby, with great credit to himself, kept his head. He explained briefly to the visitors what had happened and locked the study door, allowing nobody in, and telephoned immediately to Doctor Mason and for me. When I arrived the doctor had just concluded his examination, and this is the most extraordinary part of the case, Mr. Blackmore. The knife had penetrated beneath the shoulder blade and pierced the heart; it was, without a doubt, a fatal blow, but — ' the lawyer stopped for a moment and cleared his throat. 'Doctor Mason cannot be certain that it was actually the knife that caused Albrey's death!'

Blackmore leaned forward in his chair. 'Why?' he asked.

'Because,' said Edward Cranston, and his voice dropped almost to a whisper, 'at the time the blow was struck Doctor Mason affirms that James Albrey was suffering from the new disease which has recently made its appearance in this country and it is impossible to say whether he died from the knife wound or from the 'Purple Plague'!'

2

The Airtight Envelope

At the solicitor's words Blackmore felt a little thrill of interest run through him.

'Do you mean to say,' he exclaimed, 'that at the time James Albrey was stabbed he was either dead or dying from the 'Purple Plague'!'

'That is what Doctor Mason says,' answered Edward Cranston.

'But surely,' said John, 'he could tell which was the actual cause of death?'

'He says he can't,' the lawyer replied. 'He says that the disease has such an effect on the blood that it is impossible to be certain. He declares, however, that either way it was only a matter of minutes.'

'You mean,' queried the detective, 'that if the knife hadn't killed him the Plague would a few minutes after, or vice versa?'

The lawyer nodded.

For a moment or two Blackmore sat silent, occupied with his thoughts. Ever since the first appearance of the 'Purple Plague' he had been hoping for a chance of studying the disease at close quarters, but pressure of work had prevented him from doing so. Now it seemed that fate had thrown the opportunity in his way.

'It certainly promises to be a most interesting affair,' he remarked at length. 'I suppose you have no suspicion concerning the identity of the person who stabbed Albrey; under the circumstances we can hardly say murderer.'

The lawyer shook his head emphatically.

'Not the least.' he declared. 'So far as I know James Albrey had not an enemy in the world. Of course, like all successful men, there were many people who were envious of his wealth, but I can't think of any one who could have had any reason for killing him.'

'Of course,' said John, 'you have already informed the police?'

'I got in touch with the local police station immediately,' said Cranston, 'and they sent an inspector round at once. He was engaged in interrogating the servants when I left.'

'Has any clue been discovered up to now?' asked the detective.

'No,' answered the lawyer, shaking his head. 'The whole thing seems wrapped in mystery.'

'Who was the lady Albrey was expecting and who called so late at night?' questioned John, after a slight pause.

He noted the momentary hesitation before Cranston replied.

'Her name is Edna Lister,' he said slowly, as though carefully weighing his words. I believe Albrey had asked her to call with the intention of offering her a situation as his secretary.'

'But surely,' said John raising his eyebrows in surprise, 'it was rather a late hour for him to choose to interview an employee, particularly of the opposite sex?'

'I suppose it was,' admitted the lawyer evasively, 'but then Albrey was always rather eccentric.'

Blackmore began to feel a conviction

stealing over him that the solicitor was keeping something back. He was certain, from Cranston's manner, that the lawyer knew more about the girl and the reason for her late visit than he disclosed. He made no comment, however, but continued his questions.

'You said that she was accompanied by a young man. Who was he, and why was he there?'

There was no hesitation this time.

'I believe that he merely accompanied Miss Lister,' replied Cranston. 'After all, the hour was late and naturally — '

'I think the best thing we can do,' said Blackmore, rising quickly to his feet, 'is to get along to the scene of the crime as soon as possible. The longer we wait the less likely I can pick up any slight clue there may be. If you will excuse me for a moment I'll get my secretary to bring the car round.'

'There's no need to do that,' interposed Cranston. 'I've got mine outside and we can drive down in that.'

'Fine,' said Blackmore. 'Then if you will wait here for a few minutes while I change and collect a few things that will be necessary for my investigations we'll start at once. I won't keep you a minute.'

He went into the dining room and briefly explained to Cartwright where they were going.

A moment later the three of them were ensconced in the solicitor's big saloon and rolling swiftly along in the direction of Staines.

During the journey John gave Harry a more detailed account of the affair, and dictated a few rough notes, which the secretary took down. The run was a short one for the car was speedy and at that hour of the morning, once clear of the London streets, there was little traffic ahead of them.

Elm Lodge proved to be a large house standing in its own grounds and the only outward sign of the tragedy that had occurred within was the figure of a constable who stood on guard by the big gates leading into the drive. On seeing the car he stepped forward, evidently with the intention of stopping them, but recognising Cranston drew back and allowed it to pass unchallenged. They ran smoothly up the winding drive over a carpet of fallen leaves between an avenue of chestnuts, now but gaunt skeletons of their former selves, and presently rounding a bend drew up before a flight of steps, which was evidently the main entrance to the house.

The lawyer alighted almost before the car had come to a standstill and as he ascended the steps, closely followed by John and Cartwright, the door was opened by a little, stout, bald-headed man, who, although dressed in the conventional black of an under servant, had lost that air of quiet, old-fashioned dignity that from his appearance had seemed natural to look for, and clearly showed traces of a sleepless night in his white, haggard face, while about him was an atmosphere of suppressed agitation.

'Ah, Wilby,' said Cranston, as they entered the spacious hall, and the butler closed the door behind them. 'Has anything fresh occurred while I've been away?'

Wilby shook his head.

'No, sir,' he answered, in a voice that quivered slightly. 'Inspector Peekers has questioned all the servants and, I believe, completed his investigations. He's on the 'phone at the moment to Scotland Yard.'

'This is Mr. John Blackmore,' said the lawyer. 'I have retained him to look into this terrible affair.'

Wilby bowed.

'I hope you will be successful, sir,' he said deferentially. Cranston turned to Blackmore.

'I suppose,' he said. 'You'd like to see the study?'

'Yes,' answered John.

'Of course, Miss Lister and the young man who accompanied her are gone?' he added, turning to the butler.

'Yes, sir,' replied Wilby. 'Inspector Peekers told them that they could after he had questioned them. The young lady was very upset, and as she had to go to business this morning the inspector dealt with her first and allowed her to go home.'

'Then let's go to the study.' said John.

The butler crossed the hall, at a door

on the right of the big staircase he paused, and gently turning the handle held it open. Blackmore stopped on the threshold and looked swiftly round the room.

It was a large apartment, comfortably furnished. The walls were surrounded with dwarf bookcases, on the top of which stood several bronze statues, a collection of ivory carvings and one or two pieces of rare china. On the buff-coloured walls hung a few fine etchings. Opposite the door was a large carved, oak fireplace, drawn up in front of which was a big, roomy Chesterfield and a couple of deep saddle-bag easy chairs upholstered in golden brown leather. It was a room that showed the owner to be a man of taste. The most conspicuous piece of furniture in the place was a large, flat-topped desk of carved oak, black with age, that stood before the open French windows, which John saw led out on to a balcony.

Seated behind this, with his back to the window, was the figure of a man. His face was invisible for he sat crouched over the desk with his head resting on the blotting-pad and his arms flung out rigidly before him, the hands tightly clenched.

For some moments Blackmore remained standing beside the door, his eyes travelling swiftly over the wide expanse of carpet that lay between the door and the desk. It was of a pale brown shade, a trifle lighter than the leather that covered the furniture and was of a thick velvet pile. If he had expected to find anything here he was disappointed, for the surface of the carpet was clean and free from any speck or mark.

Having finished his preliminary scrutiny the detective advanced to the desk and bent over the grim object, which lay across it. He looked at it for a second or two in silence and then turned to Cranston.

'Is this the exact position in which you found him?' he enquired.

The butler answered before the lawyer had time to reply.

'Yes sir,' he said from his position by the door. 'He hasn't been moved.

Inspector Peekers did, however, remove the knife.'

John nodded and his eyes rested for a moment on the narrow slit in the black dinner jacket between the shoulders that was surrounded by an ominous stain. For some seconds he remained in this position, staring at the picture before him. Turning, he gazed out through the open French window across the lawn to a belt of shrubbery beyond. Presently, without turning his head and with his eyes still fixed on the garden, he suddenly addressed a question to the butler:

'When you made the discovery, Wilby, was the window open or closed?'

'It was open,' replied Wilby, without hesitation. 'Mr. Albrey was very fond of fresh air, sir, and, winter or summer, he always insisted on having his windows open both here and in his bedroom.'

John nodded and allowed his eyes to drop to the floor. The chair upon which the dead man was seated stood upon a Persian rug. Between this and the window there was nothing but a strip of highly polished boards, the distance being slightly less than three feet. He stooped and closely examined the intervening space between the window and the rug but there was not the slightest sign of a mark of any description. He stepped out on to the balcony and looked about him and then suddenly, with a little exclamation, he dropped on to one knee and peered closely at the stonework.

The marks that had attracted his attention were faint and might easily have passed unnoticed. There were several of them and they were in the shape of half moons. John followed them with his eyes and saw that they led along the balcony to a flight of steps that went down to a gravel path to the side of the lawn. The marks themselves had been made by a thin film of damp mud, and even while John was looking at them they were rapidly drying. In another half hour or so, when the sun's rays had worked their way round to that side of the house they would practically, completely disappear. It was impossible to mistake their significance, and Blackmore's eyes gleamed with satisfaction. Someone had obviously approached the window on tiptoe, and it was fairly logical to conclude that that someone was the person who had stabbed James Albrey. It was hardly likely that anyone else would have had any object in concealing their movements by tiptoeing along the balcony like that.

Blackmore searched in his pockets and produced an envelope. From this he withdrew a sheet of thin tracing paper. It was of a peculiar quality and he had it specially made for the purpose for which he was about to use it. It was one of the several things he had taken from the drawer in his desk before leaving Mecklinburg Square.

Selecting the clearest and most sharply defined of the prints he knelt down, and with infinite care proceeded to make a tracing, indicating even the position of the nail marks round the edge. The shoes that had made the print were of rather a peculiar shape, the toes being extraordinarily broad, and the tracing that he was making would be invaluable as a means of identification when the person who had walked along the balcony was eventually discovered. Having finished it, and placing the tracing carefully in his pocket, John rose and returned to the room of death.

Inspector Peekers had joined the others during his absence on the balcony and was talking in a low tone to Cartwright and the lawyer. He came forward to greet John as he stepped through the window.

Peekers was a tall, military-looking man, clean shaven, and with a face that looked as if it had been carved from a block of hard and exceptionally well-seasoned teak with a very blunt hatchet. John liked him the moment he saw him.

'Very glad to know you, Mr. Blackmore,' he exclaimed in a pleasant voice as they shook hands. 'I've never been fortunate to run up against you before because of business, and I'm looking forward to working with you in this case. It seems a most extraordinary affair. I must say that I'm completely in the dark.'

'I agree that at the moment it does appear rather puzzling,' said John, 'but it's too early yet to form an opinion. You have, I understand, already questioned the servants?'

'Yes,' answered the inspector, 'but there's nothing to be learnt from them.'

'What about the two people who made the discovery with Wilby; have they got anything to say?'

'Nothing of any importance,' said Peekers. 'The girl, whose name is Edna Lister, is employed as a cashier at Messrs. Belbridge's, in Oxford Street. She says that she received a letter from James Albrey three days ago, asking her to call and see him at eleven o'clock on the evening of September the eighth — that was last night — with reference to a situation as secretary. She was very surprised because she says she does not know Albrey, and at first she made up her mind to take no notice of the letter. After thinking it over, however, she came to the conclusion that it might possibly offer her a chance of getting a better situation than she held at Belbridge's, and decided, after talking the matter over with her fiancé, to keep the appointment. The hour mentioned seemed such a strange one that her fiancé, his name, by the way, is Frank Holland and he works for a firm of hardware merchants in Leadenhall Street, insisted on accompanying her. And that's all they appear to know about the matter.'

John made a noncommittal reply. During the inspector's brief recital he had been carefully watching Edward Cranston. At the mention of Edna Lister's name he had distinctly noticed a vague look of troubled uneasiness spread over the lawyer's rubicund face. What was it that Cranston was keeping back? he thought. That the solicitor was withholding something he was sure, and he determined to tackle him at the first opportunity, and, if possible, find out what it was. At the moment, however, he decided to say nothing.

'I've got the knife,' continued Peekers, 'and I'm sending it up to Scotland Yard to be tested for fingerprints, though I'm doubtful whether it's going to help us very much, because, from the rapid examination I made of the hilt I'm rather under the impression that the murderer wore gloves. Would you like to see it?'

John shook his head.

'No, I don't think it's necessary,' he replied. 'I can always see it at the Yard if it should be. Doctor Mason wasn't able to say definitely that it was the knife that actually caused Albrey's death, was he?' he added.

Peekers shook his head.

'No,' he replied. 'That point appeared to be rather a knotty one. He says that Albrey exhibited every symptom of having been suffering from this new disease, the 'Purple Plague' at the time he met his death, and that, as far as the medical evidence is concerned, it would be impossible to state definitely whether he died from the result of the disease or from the knife wound. It's the most extraordinary case I've ever struck. The man has, apparently, in all respects been killed twice. Why he should have been stabbed when be was already dead or dying from the 'Purple Plague' is a mystery.'

'I don't think the explanation of that is very far to seek,' said John. 'I'm of the opinion that the person who stabbed

Albrey was unaware at the time that he was suffering from the disease.'

Peekers looked at him sharply.

'What exactly do you mean?' he enquired.

'Have you examined the balcony outside the window?' asked Blackmore, with apparent irrelevance.

'Yes,' replied Peekers, 'but I didn't find anything important.'

'If you'll look more closely,' said John, 'you'll find several toe-prints on the stone flags. They're very faint, certainly, I don't suppose I should have seen them if I hadn't been looking for them.'

The inspector looked rather surprised.

'Looking for?' put in Cranston, in astonishment. 'Do you mean to say you expected to find them?'

John nodded.

'Yes,' he replied. 'The moment I entered this room and saw the position of the body, and the open window, it struck me immediately that in all probability Albrey had been stabbed from the balcony outside. I immediately sought for traces and found the footprints. They clearly indicate that some one had approached from the garden and tiptoed along the balcony as far as the window. There are also indications that he or she returned the same way. I haven't yet examined the path that runs along the foot of the balcony steps, but I intend to do so later. In the meanwhile I should like to ask Wilby one or two questions.'

The butler, who had been standing nervously in the doorway during the whole of John's investigations, looked up at the mention of his name.

'Now, Wilby,' began Blackmore gently, 'first of all can you tell us whether your master was in his usual state of health yesterday?'

'Yes, sir,' answered the butler without hesitation. 'In fact he seemed to be brighter and more cheerful than usual.'

'Did he have any visitors during the day?' continued the detective.

'Not until just after dinner,' answered Wilby, 'when a man, who I've never seen before, called and asked to see him. He wouldn't give me any name and asked me to take a note in to Mr. Albrey.'

'And your master was quite well then?' asked John.

'Yes, sir,' said Wilby. 'Quite well.'

'Where was he sitting?'

'He was sitting behind his desk, writing letters. It wasn't until later that he complained of feeling unwell.'

'Oh, he did complain of feeling unwell?' said John sharply, and shot a quick glance at Cartwright. 'When was that?'

'After the man — the stranger had gone, sir, when I took him in his coffee.'

Blackmore paused for a moment, thoughtfully.

'Did he open the note in your presence,' he went on.

Wilby nodded.

'Yes, sir,' he said. 'He read it through. It seemed quite a short note and he said 'Good God!' and muttered something else below his breath that I didn't catch, and asked me to show the man in.'

'I gather from what you say that he seemed surprised,' said John.

'Yes, he seemed very surprised, sir, and rather agitated I thought.'

'And you've never seen this man before?'

'Never,' replied the butler emphatically. 'I've never seen him before in my life.'

'What was he like?' asked John. 'Can you describe him?'

Wilby's grey brows met in a straight line across his forehead as he strove to concentrate his thoughts.

'Well, he's rather difficult to describe, sir,' he answered at last. 'He was quite a gentleman, though. Wore a light fawn overcoat and a soft hat, the hat was pulled over his eyes and he kept a white muffler he wore closely round his chin, so that I couldn't see very much of his face. But he was tall and rather thin.'

'Would you be able to recognise him again?' asked John.

'I'm afraid I shouldn't, sir,' said Wilby, slowly shaking his head. 'Not unless he was dressed the same.'

'How long was he with your master?'

'About twenty minutes,' said the butler. 'Might have been a little less but it certainly wasn't more.'

'I understand,' said John, 'that during

the interview you passed the study door on your way to the kitchen from the dining room and heard voices raised in altercation. Do you mean that they were quarrelling?'

'Yes, sir, they were.'

'Could you distinguish anything that was said?'

'I heard the master say 'You'll get nothing out of me, you scoundrel, not a penny'.'

'Is that all you heard?'

'Yes, sir. I didn't stop to listen,' replied Wilby with dignity.

'And then the man left shortly after?'

'Yes, sir, I saw him let himself out as I came back from the kitchen with the coffee.'

'And it was when you brought the coffee in to your master that he complained of feeling unwell?'

'Yes, sir,' replied Wilby. 'He was white and trembling, and said he felt rather dizzy. I asked if I could do anything, but he said that it would pass off in a moment and that he didn't want to be disturbed. He told me that he was expecting a lady at eleven o'clock and when she came I was to show her straight in.'

'And you didn't see him again until you made the discovery of his death?' asked John.

'No, sir.'

Blackmore paused and rubbed his chin.

'Has the note referred to by Wilby been found?' he asked, looking at Inspector Peekers.

The Inspector reddened slightly.

'To tell you the truth, Mr. Blackmore,' he said, 'I never gave it a thought. It seemed so obvious that the man who called could have nothing to do with the affair since he was alive after he left that I didn't attach much importance to the note.'

'I think it would be as well all the same,' said John, 'to see if we can find it.'

He crossed to the desk and commenced to search hastily but methodically among the mass of documents that littered the broad surface. Peekers went to his aid, and together they examined the pile of papers, while Cartwright and the lawyer were interestedly looking on.

'There doesn't appear to be a sign of it here,' said John, shaking his head when the last paper had been looked at. 'There's a possibility he might have thrust it into one of these drawers, we'd better make sure.'

'Perhaps it's under the body' suggested Harry.

'We can soon see,' replied John. 'Give me a hand, will you, Peekers?'

Together they raised the limp form and as they did so Cartwright uttered an exclamation and darted quickly forward. On the blotting pad where the head had rested lay an envelope.

'Here it is,' said Harry triumphantly. A second later he gave a little exclamation of disappointment. 'It's empty,' he said disgustedly.

Making sure that there was nothing else concealed beneath they lowered the body back again into its original position on the desk. John came over and took the envelope from his secretary's hand.

It was a white envelope of a good quality and a shape that is generally known as 'business size'. John scrutinised the outside carefully and raising the flap peered into the interior. As he did so his brows puckered up into a puzzled frown.

'What is it?' asked Cartwright eagerly.

'This envelope is a most peculiar one,' said Blackmore, shaking his head. 'I don't think I've ever come across one like it before.'

Inspector Peekers stepped quickly across to his side.

'What is there peculiar about it?' he asked.

'It appears to be lined with an inner covering of fine oilskin,' said John slowly. 'Look!'

He opened the flap and the others craned forward as he pointed to the interior of the envelope. It was in reality two in one, the outer covering consisted of ordinary stiff paper of the kind which better class stationery is made from, inside that was a second envelope of fine oilskin, fitting closely like the lining of a glove.

'It's most extraordinary,' said Cranston. 'I certainly have never seen anything like it before.'

'Nor I,' said the inspector. 'I wonder what the object could have been?'

'That's easily understandable,' replied John, and there was such a note of excitement in his voice that Harry looked at him quickly. 'The object is quite obviously to render the envelope airtight,' continued Blackmore. 'You see, when the flap is stuck down the interior becomes hermetically sealed.'

'But why should anyone go to all that trouble and expense?' asked Peekers in a puzzled voice. 'What advantage is there in using an envelope that is airtight?'

'It depends entirely on the contents,' murmured John abstractedly, still turning the envelope over in his fingers. Suddenly he held it out to Wilby. 'Is this the same envelope that you took in to your master?'

The butler advanced and looked at it.

'Yes, sir,' he said. 'It's the same one.'

'It's curious,' said John, 'that we can't find the note it contained. It must be here somewhere, we'd better have another look.'

But though they searched everywhere, the drawers of the desk, the knee space beneath, every conceivable place where it was possible for the note to have been put, there was no sign of it. Blackmore even examined the dead ashes of the fire, on the chance that it might have been burnt, but there was no trace of charred paper in the grate.

'There is only one explanation,' he said at length, when they had completed their search, 'and that is that the stranger took it away with him.'

'But why?' asked Cartwright.

John shrugged his shoulders.

'There are several explanations,' he replied, 'the most probable being that it was signed with his name and he didn't want anyone to discover it.'

'In that case he must have known — ' began Inspector Peekers, when he was interrupted by a loud knocking on the front door.

Wilby hurried away to answer the summons, and a moment later returned to say that an ambulance had arrived to convey all that remained of James Albrey to the mortuary to await the inquest.

'Just one moment,' said John. 'I should

like to examine the body before it is removed.' He crossed over to the still form and commenced his grim task.

The doctor, in making his examination, had previously loosened the white collar, and as Blackmore reverently raised the head Cartwright saw that the ghastly rash which was one of the chief characteristics of that dreadful plague covered the neck and face of the dead man. The mauve lines, like a spider's web, stood out visibly against the dead white of the set features. It was indescribably horrible, and the secretary could scarcely suppress a shudder as he saw it. Apparently it had no such effect on his employer, for with calm detachment he peered closely at the dead man, noting carefully the position of the knife wound between the shoulder blades, the clothing, and paying particular care to the bloodstains surrounding the slit in the cloth of the dinner jacket.

Presently he came to the hands, still clenched in the last death agony, and bending closely over them submitted them to a long scrutiny. The rash had evidently not extended to the hands, for the backs were white and entirely free from any blemish. They were clasped loosely and John gently unclosed the fingers. As he did so Cartwright, who was nearest, heard him draw in his breath sharply.

'What is it?' he asked. 'What have you found?' But he might as well have been speaking to a stone image for all the notice Blackmore took of his question. Truth to tell, he had not even heard him, for the unclosing of those dead fingers had revealed the fact that the tip of each was strangely swollen and was the same horrible mauve hue as the rash that covered the face. It was particularly noticeable on the inside of the thumb and first finger, and as John's brain suggested to him a possible explanation a conviction took possession of him that the outbreak of the mysterious disease which had baffled the medical profession throughout the country was not due to natural causes after all!

3

The Scrap of Torn Paper

It was a startling thought, almost too far fetched to be given credence, and yet it was a theory that admitted all the facts. It accounted for the spasmodic and isolated fatalities, an aspect that had so puzzled the doctors. If John was right and the 'Purple Plague' was not due to an unknown foreign disease as was believed, but was the outcome of some diabolical brain that was directing and using it for its own purpose then several hitherto unexplainable incidents connected with it suddenly became clear. The strange fact that only one person in each locality had been stricken by the malady was easily understandable. At the same time, Blackmore's theory was founded on such a slender basis that he decided to keep it to himself till such time as irrefutable proof was forthcoming to substantiate his idea.

He made up his mind to enquire closely into the previous deaths that had occurred as the result of the plague as soon as possible, and see if he could light on some clue that would confirm his suspicions. If the 'Purple Plague' were indeed being used by some human intelligence then there must be some deep, underlying motive behind it, unless the whole thing was the work of a madman. Blackmore determined to discover what that motive was.

The death of James Albrey could be but an incident in the scheme since the disease had made its appearance two months prior to its occurrence. There was, of course, the probability that John was wrong in his suspicions, which had first been aroused by the peculiar construction of the envelope containing the note that had been delivered to the millionaire. The moment he had seen it and discovered the oilskin lining, he had been convinced the envelope had been intended for quite a different purpose than to become the receptacle for the note that it had contained. Exactly what that purpose was, he was, for the moment, unable to conjecture, but for some reason he was certain that it was connected with the 'Purple Plague'.

He found it difficult, even to himself, to account for his theory that the disease had been brought about by some human agency, the very flimsy fact on which he had based this sudden suspicion seemed totally inadequate, but at the same time he could not put the idea out of his brain. A sixth sense and an inner voice seemed to be whispering to him that he was right.

As he straightened up from his examination of the dead man's fingers Inspector Peekers, who had been interestedly watching, came a step forward.

'Have you discovered anything?' he asked.

'Nothing definite,' replied John. 'There is no reason why the ambulance men should not proceed with their work. While they are arranging for the removal of the body,' he added, turning to Cranston, 'I should like to have a few words with you. Is there anywhere where we can talk privately?'

'Yes, Mr. Blackmore,' answered the lawyer, 'we can go into the dining room.'

'That'll do,' said the detective. 'I'll see you in a moment, Cartwright,' he said, turning to his secretary.

They stood aside at the door to allow the two men who were entering with the stretcher to pass, and then went out into the hall. Cranston led the way to a door almost opposite the study. Opening it he signed for John to precede him into the room.

It was a large room with oak panelled walls, against one of which stood a massive sideboard, laden with silver. Down the centre ran a long polished table, in the middle of which was a big china bowl filled with white chrysanthemums.

'What is it you wish to speak to me about, Mr. Blackmore?' asked Cranston as he closed the door and came over to the other side.

John looked at him for a moment in silence.

'Mr. Cranston,' he began, after a slight pause, 'there are several questions I should like to ask you. In a case of this description one of the first things to seek is a motive, and the motive for murder must necessarily be a strong one. You have already informed me that you and Albrey were great friends. To your knowledge, is there anything in his life that is likely to throw any light on the reason for his death?'

'No,' answered the lawyer, shaking his head. 'As I have already told you, the whole thing is a complete mystery to me.'

'Then you haven't the least suspicion,' said John, eyeing him keenly, 'of any one who is likely to benefit at all by putting Albrey out of the way? For instance, I presume he has made a will, and being his legal advisor you of course know the contents of that will. To whom does his property pass?'

Cranston hesitated so long before replying that John repeated his question.

'Mr. Blackmore,' he said, in a low, hesitating voice, 'I wish to do everything in my power, as you must be aware, to help to bring to justice the person responsible for my poor friend's death, but in answering your question I shall be breaking a confidence. Can I rely on the fact that anything I tell you will remain strictly, between ourselves, that you will not let it go further than this room?'

John considered for a moment or two and then he nodded.

'Provided that it doesn't interfere with the interests of justice,' he replied, 'you can rest assured that anything you tell me will be treated with strict confidence.'

'Very well then,' said the lawyer. 'You asked me just now who benefits by the terms of Albrey's will, I'll tell you. Edna Lister is the sole legatee!'

Blackmore was accustomed to receiving surprises but he could not suppress the start of astonishment that he gave at Cranston's words.

'Edna Lister?' he echoed in amazement. 'That was the girl who called to see Albrey on the night of his death?'

'Precisely,' answered Cranston. 'She inherits the entire fortune.'

'Does she know?' asked John.

The lawyer shook his head.

'No,' he replied. 'Neither will she know

for some time.' He paused and then apparently making up his mind continued; 'It's rather an extraordinary complication, Mr. Blackmore. Having told you so much I might as well tell you the whole story.

'Three days ago Albrey sent for me asking me to come and dine with him. He said he had an important matter of business, which he wished to talk over. He then told me a story, which, friendly as I have been with him, I had never heard before. When Albrey's father died he left over a hundred thousand pounds to be divided equally between James Albrey and his sister, Grace. She was younger than Albrey, barely twenty at the time, and because she had the money she attracted to her some of the worst men it was possible to find in London. Out of this bunch of flotsam and jetsam she chose the worst of the worst.' Cranston stopped speaking to get his breath. 'She married a plausible villain who eventually ruined her, and then left her with a mountain of debts. Eight months after they were married he ran away, leaving her penniless, broken in both pocket and spirit. Her health, which had never been too good, gave under the strain and a month later she died giving birth to a child, a girl. She was ashamed to communicate with her brother, and it was not until some months after that he learned of her death. She had died in great poverty and none knew what had become of the baby. Albrey told me he had spent large sums in trying to trace the child, and eventually he succeeded. He succeeded just a week before he sent for me and told me the story. He discovered that she was working as a cashier at Belbridge's, in Oxford Street, under the name of Edna Lister. Being a bachelor, without kith or kin — there was a younger brother but he died years previously in Canada — Albrey told me that he wished to have a will drawn up which made this girl, his niece, his sole heiress. 'But, Cranston,' he said, 'there is a condition I want you to include in the will. She is to know nothing about it until after such time as she is married. I'm not going to risk the same thing happening to her kid as it did with poor Grace. I'm going to write to her,' he continued, 'and offer her a position with me as private secretary; in this way I shall be able to keep an eye on her and see that she has several little luxuries that I should like her to have. But she will never know that I am her uncle or that I am in any way related until, as I state, she is happily married, and I know that there is no risk of some scoundrel being attracted to her on account of the money.' That's the story, Mr. Blackmore, and I confess at the time I was astonished. Although I had known Albrey from boyhood it was the first time he had ever taken me into his confidence regarding his sister. I knew that she had died somewhere abroad, but that was all.'

'It's an extraordinary story,' declared John. 'I can quite understand Albrey's point of view. Had it been known that the girl was his heiress it would have brought all the adventurers in the country buzzing about her ears. But what about the will, was it executed?'

The lawyer nodded.

'Yes,' he answered. 'I had it drawn up

the next day and brought it round in the evening for Albrey to sign. He signed it in the presence of Wilby and one of the maids, who acted as witnesses. In any case, even if the will had not been signed his money would have passed to Edna Lister, provided she could have proved that she was his niece. She is the next of kin.'

The detective's brows were puckered in a thoughtful frown.

'What happened to the husband?' he enquired. 'The man who deserted Albrey's sister?'

Cranston shrugged his shoulders.

'He was never heard of again,' he declared. 'Albrey told me he tried vainly to find him but without success.'

'And there is no other relation?' asked John. 'No distant cousin to whom the money would go in the event of anything happening to the girl?'

'No,' said Cranston. 'No one. As I said just now, there was a younger brother, Bertram Albrey, but he died three years ago in Canada. Of course, had he been still alive, and there was no will, he would get the money, automatically, as the next of kin.'

'I suppose there is no doubt about his death?' said John.

Cranston shook his head.

'I don't think there's the slightest,' he declared. 'He was killed as the result of a brawl in some gambling den in Montreal. I believe he had always been the black sheep of the family and was in prison twice before he was thirty for forgery. I think the news of his death was a relief to Albrey, for he was always sending him money and getting him out of scrapes. Altogether Bertram was rather a responsibility to him.'

'You're quite sure that Edna Lister has no knowledge of the fact that she is Albrey's heiress?' asked John.

'Perfectly certain,' replied Cranston, emphatically. 'Albrey told no one but me, and naturally you are the first person I have mentioned it to, seeing that he told it to me in the strictest confidence.'

Blackmore shook his head with a puzzled frown.

'It doesn't help matters much,' he said.

'I was hoping that possibly I could light on some motive that would enable us to identify the person who stabbed him, but even there we are up against a dead wall for we cannot say definitely that he died from the result of the knife wound. In fact it is the strangest case I've ever tackled. I can't think of one that is parallel to it.'

The lawyer was on the point of replying when there came a tap at the door and Cartwright entered.

'Excuse me,' he said. 'The ambulance has gone and Inspector Peekers would like to see you for a moment.'

With a word of apology to the lawyer John followed his secretary out into the hall.

The Inspector was standing by the front door, evidently on the point of departure.

'I'm just off,' he said, as John crossed over to him. 'I'm going down to the station to make out my report. I've left a constable and a sergeant in charge and I've instructed them not to interfere with you in any way.'

John thanked him.

'I hope, Mr. Blackmore,' said the Inspector as he shook hands in farewell, 'you'll let me know if you discover anything. This is the first big case I've ever handled and I'm anxious to make good.'

'I can assure you, Peekers,' said the detective, 'that directly I've got anything definite I'll let you know at once. At the present moment I'm as much in the dark as you are.'

With a word of thanks the Inspector hurried away.

'What do we do now?' asked Cartwright, as John turned and slowly crossed the hall.

'Not much we can do,' replied his employer, with a slight shrug of his shoulders. 'At the moment we appear to be at a dead end. I think we'll just have a look at the path that runs along at the foot of the balcony steps in case there's anything we've overlooked, and then get back home. There are one or two important enquiries I want to put in motion.'

He opened the door of the study, now

devoid of its former grim occupant, and crossed over to the French windows. Hurrying along the balcony he ran swiftly down the steps to the gravel path that stretched completely round the house and passing between two high yew hedges joined the main drive at the front. John's eyes searched the moist surface, but he soon saw that all hope of following the tracks of the footprints he had discovered on the balcony was futile. There were footprints in plenty but such a confused jumble that it was useless looking for any particular one.

'No good,' he said, pausing disappointedly. 'There's nothing to be learned here, and we may as well retrace our steps.'

They were about to ascend to the balcony again when Cartwright gave a little exclamation and hurried forward to a point some three yards up the path. A little speck of white lying in a hollow where the grass bordered the gravel had caught his eye. Reaching the place he stooped and picked it up. It was a little ball of paper, creased and crumpled and discoloured. He smoothed it out and saw several lines of pencilled writing, almost indecipherable, scribbled on it.

'What do you make of this?' he asked excitedly, hurrying back to where John was standing.

His employer took the paper and after some difficulty managed to make out a few lines that had been scrawled across it. Some of them were impossible to read for they had been written with a soft pencil and the writing had got rubbed out. Those that were visible were as follows:

. . . in the wall . . . Thursday . . . eight-thirty . . . Zat . . .

John's eyes sparkled as he folded the paper and put it away in his pocketbook.

'What is it?' asked Cartwright.

'The first tangible clue we've struck so far,' replied Blackmore. 'Unless I'm mistaken 'In the wall' refers to a place called the 'Hole in the Wall' in Penny-fields, and one of the worst dens in the East End of London. This paper is obviously a message fixing an appoint-ment there for Thursday. Tomorrow is Thursday, and tomorrow night we shall also be present to see who keeps the appointment, because I'm inclined to think the person this note was sent to is the person who stabbed James Albrey!'

4

The Hole in the Wall

A night mist, raw and penetrating, hung over the Thames and encroached hesitantly into the narrow byways and alleys that stretch away from the lighted thoroughfare that runs through Penny-fields and lose themselves eventually in the darkness, which is cast by the shadows of the tall, ramshackle warehouses that line the left bank of the river.

Along a street, on each side of which clustered barrows lit with flaring naptha lamps, two figures were shuffling at a rapid pace; taking no notice of the cosmopolitan crowd of mixed nationalities with whom they jostled shoulders. The bigger of the two presented the appearance of a stoker of some merchant vessel, while the shorter figure by his side could easily have been the engineer of the same ship. Certainly no one would ever have suspected that their rough exteriors concealed the identities of John Blackmore and his secretary, for the disguise was perfect to the last detail.

John's time had been fully occupied since leaving Elm Lodge on the previous day. After completing his investigations and taking leave of Edward Cranston he had returned home and spent the rest of the afternoon seated at his desk busily writing. The result of his labours had been a batch of letters and telegrams, the addresses of some of which caused Cartwright to open his eyes wide with astonishment. But though the secretary had started by firing a volley of questions at his master almost as soon as they had left the house at Staines he had in the end given it up in despair, although he was consumed by an overpowering curiosity. On occasions John Blackmore could be as close as the proverbial oyster and he had skilfully parried all Cartwright's enquiries with evasive answers.

Several replies to the telegrams had been received that morning and John spent the day, until it was time to leave for Pennyfields, poring over their contents.

'What do you expect to find at the 'Hole in the Wall?' asked Cartwright, as they climbed down a narrow, ill-lighted alley in which the mist seemed to have settled in dense packets, so that now and again they had to slacken speed and almost grope their way.

John paused and stepped aside to avoid a drunken Lascar sailor who suddenly swayed in front of his path.

'I hope to discover some clue to the identity of the person who stabbed Albrey.' he answered.

'Yes, I know that,' said Harry. 'But how do you expect to be able to recognize the man the message was sent to? There's sure to be a fairly big crowd there and I don't see how you intend to pick out one man out of all that lot?'

'Quite easily,' said Blackmore. 'You seem to forget the toe-print.'

'You mean the toe-print on the balcony,' said Cartwright. 'How are they going to help you?'

'They're going to help a lot, answered

66

John with a chuckle. 'The shoes that made those prints are not an ordinary pair by any means. Provided that they were made to fit the foot of the person who was wearing them I don't think there's much doubt of that, there'll be little difficulty in picking him out from among a thousand.'

'How do you mean?' asked the secretary curiously, looking up as they passed under the dim glow of the street lamp.

'The width of the toes,' replied John. 'I don't suppose there's one man in a hundred with such a wide foot, so abnormal as to suggest deformity.' He broke off to give a direction. 'We turn to the right here — down that alley.'

They swung into a black opening between the broken stone walls of two large buildings that were apparently factories into an evil smelling passageway that was so narrow it was almost impossible for the two of them to walk abreast. It was lighted dimly at irregular intervals by dilapidated gas lamps, that projected from the walls on rusty iron brackets.

The white mist was getting thicker, and Cartwright guessed by this that they were penetrating nearer to the river. Air, too, began to become redolent of that mixture of odours which is a combination of tarred ropes, rotting planking, and the salty tang of the seawater that gives rise to a smell that is totally indescribable, but can be experienced by anyone taking a walk near the wharfs of the Thames.

At the end of the passage way they crossed a cobbled road and plunged immediately into another that was, if anything, darker and more noisome than the first.

'It's a good job we know this locality well,' said John. 'It would be easy enough to get lost round here, specially in this confounded fog.'

'It's getting so thick,' said Cartwright shivering, 'that it's almost impossible to see one's hand before one's face.'

Halfway along the passage they blundered into the shuffling figure of a Chinaman, and Blackmore cursed him heartily, true to the type he was representing.

'We're nearly there now,' he remarked, as the sound of the Chinaman's footsteps had faded in the distance.

The passage led out into a broad street, that is to say it was broad in comparison to the narrow alley they had just left, and John turned sharply to the right. The fog was patchy, and here it had thinned slightly, so that on the opposite side of the roadway between the tall buildings that fringed the street could be vaguely glimpsed the shadowy outline of anchored vessels on the river, their mast lights making watery, streaky glimmers in the swirling vapour.

About two hundred yards along John slowed down. In front of them there burst through the fog a garish blaze of light, in the hazy radiance of which they could dimly see little groups of shadowy figures, indistinct and distorted. Presently they passed a public house, from the interior of which came the sound of clinking glasses interspersed with rough oaths and sudden burst of rough laughter. They had come now to an ill-lighted part of the street, and a place where the roadway was considerably narrower. One side was flanked by some sort of tumbledown factory and the other with a few dirty and mean-looking shops. Up by the fourth of these, a cheap eating house, in the window of which was displayed an unappetizing steak surrounded by several sickly-looking tomatoes, John stopped.

'Here we are,' he whispered and pointed to the facia of the shop which could be seen in the light of the street lamp that stood almost outside.

Faintly, in the wreath of the mists that circled it Cartwright read the name inscribed in faded red letters: 'The Hole in the Wall'.

'Come on,' said John, 'and for the Lord's sake keep your wits about you. A false move and we stand very little chance of coming out alive. 'Flimsy' Harris's is about the worst joint round these parts, or anywhere else for that matter.'

By the side of the shop ran a narrow entry and John led the way down it. Half way along he stopped before a door set flush with the sidewall. Raising his hand he felt for and found the bell button in the brickwork at the side, he pressed it, two long pushes and three short ones.

There was a long interval of silence and then from within came the sound of heavy footsteps on bare boards and the door was opened to the extent of but two or three inches.

'What yer want?' growled a voice, thickly.

'Lodgin's,' grunted John.

''Ow much can yer pay?' said the voice throatily.

'Depends what the bed's like,' replied Blackmore, and Cartwright realized that the conversation must have formed some sort of a password, for the door was immediately opened wide.

'Come in,' said the man who stood on the threshold, and then catching sight of Cartwright. 'What about yer pal?'

''E's all right,' answered John. ''E's one of us.'

The man nodded and stood aside, and they stepped through the doorway into the passage beyond.

It was dimly lighted by a single flaring

gas jet and Harry saw that it was entirely devoid of even a stick of furniture.

Without another word, the man who had admitted them closed the door, preceded them down the passage to another at the end. He was a bestial-looking brute, with a coarse, bloated face, unshaven and inflamed with strong drink. He opened the door and held it while they passed through.

Beyond was a covered alleyway, at the end of which was a third door. As they drew near to it Cartwright saw, to his surprise, that this was made of iron. Their guide took a key from his pocket and inserting it in an almost invisible keyhole near the bottom of the door turned it with a sharp twist of his wrist. A pull and the door opened slowly. As it did so there came suddenly to their ears a loud babel of voices.

'Go in,' growled the man, thrusting the key back in his pocket, and Blackmore and Cartwright stepped across the threshold.

The door swung to behind them as they did so and closed with a click.

Evidently, thought the secretary, it locked with a spring.

The room in which they found themselves was large and lofty and at some time or other had, in all probability, been built for the purpose of store place, or factory. The walls were of plain, whitewashed brick and no attempt had been made to decorate the place in any way. The roof was supported on crisscross iron girders, and in the centre was a huge glass skylight, a few panes of which were missing or broken. The floor was of bare concrete and filthily dirty, littered in every direction with countless cigarette ends and matches that had been carelessly thrown down by the habitués of the place. Grouped thickly about were a number of rough deal tables and chairs, while at one end was a kind of bar that consisted simply of several tables set closely together and kept in position by a plank, that had been nailed along the side. A more sordid or filthy hole it would be difficult to imagine, and the little knots of people of both sexes that sat at the tables or lounged round the bar were on a par with the rest of the establishment.

Some were well dressed, in a flashy, vulgar way, while others appeared to be in the last stages of poverty. On the faces of all was stamped the habitual expression that marks the lower type of criminal, expressions in which, vice, greed, and sensuality struggled for mastery. Here were men from all nations, Chinamen, drinking and laughing with Sepoys, Lascars and Hindoos, blacks and a large sprinkling of whites.

In one corner were a little group clustered about a bedraggled woman, laughing coarsely at some remark she had evidently just made. At a table near the door through which they had just entered, a huge black man with a vivid scar that reached from his right eye to the point of his chin sat in close conversation with a girl who might have been pretty but for her obviously dyed hair and over-painted face, and the hard lines about her mouth and eyes.

The atmosphere was thick with smoke and fetid with the smell of stale drink. Beyond one or two who casually glanced in their direction nobody took any notice of the newcomers and Blackmore lurched forward towards an empty table that stood in close proximity to the bar, followed by Cartwright.

He beckoned to a dirty and pasty-faced youth who appeared to be acting as a kind of pot-man, and gruffly ordered two glasses of rum. When these had been brought he flung himself back in his chair and allowed his eyes to travel round the miscellaneous collection of humanity with which the place was more than half full.

'What a beastly hole,' muttered Cartwright, surveying the scene about him with a look of disgust, which, try as he would he could not keep from showing in his eyes.

'Be careful,' warned John, as he picked up his glass and took a draught from the contents, smacking his lips with feigned enjoyment, though the potent, unmatured spirit burned his throat and almost made him choke. 'Don't speak so loud.'

'Sorry,' said the secretary, lowering his voice. Speaking in a scarcely audible whisper: 'We're going to have all our work cut out to spot the man we want among this lot.'

'You're right,' answered John, with keen eyes, under the artistically swollen lids, swiftly passing from group to group and closely scrutinising each in turn. 'Not going to be easy, but I'm hoping that if we wait a little we may pick up some scraps of conversation that will make our task easier.' He glanced over to the cheap alarm clock that ticked noisily on a shelf by the rude bar. 'Barely twenty-past-eight yet, and in all probability the person we're seeking has not arrived.'

He had scarcely uttered the words when the iron door through which they had made their entrance, began to open slowly, and a man entered.

He was of medium height, dressed in a dark overcoat, evidently a new one. A cloth cap was pulled down over his eyes but not low enough to conceal his face, which showed up distinctly in the raw, unshaded light, which illumined the room from a powerful cluster hung from one of the iron girders that crossed the ceiling. He might have been good-looking, save for the signs of dissipation which marked the face and the fact that his nose had, at some time or other, been broken and badly set, so that it was crooked and twisted over to the right of his face.

Blackmore, who had taken in every detail of the man's appearance, felt his heart beat a trifle quicker, and nudged his secretary's arm.

'Look at his shoes,' he murmured.

Cartwright did so, and caught his breath, for the man's shoes, although well made, were an extraordinary shape, being particularly broad across the tread, so that the toe part was rendered almost square.

'Do you think he's the man we're looking for?' he whispered excitedly.

'Yes,' answered John in the same voice. 'Don't talk now, watch!'

The man with the broken nose had paused on the threshold of the room and was looking about him, as though in search of someone. It became clear, however, that the person for whom he was seeking was not there, for after a little while he began to make his way slowly in the direction of the bar.

A group of men who had been laughing and talking turned as he approached and one of their number came forward to meet him.

'Hello, Bertram,' he greeted, slapping the newcomer on the back. 'You're early tonight. What are you going to have?'

'Hadn't we better get nearer?' whispered Cartwright. 'We shan't be able to hear much this distance away.'

But John made no reply, as a matter of fact he had not even heard the question, for the mention of the newcomer's name had sent his thoughts back to his conversation with Edward Cranston, in the dining room of Elm Lodge the previous day. James Albrey's younger brother who was supposed to have died in Montreal three years ago was named Bertram, and John was wondering whether it was merely a coincidence or whether Bertram Albrey was alive after all!

5

A Fight for Life

Blackmore's brain worked quickly. It might after all be only coincidence that the two names were the same, but if it were not then one of the most inexplicable parts of the whole affair, namely the motive for the stabbing of the millionaire, was clear. If Albrey's brother had not died after all as was generally supposed, if the report had been a false one, then he had a very good reason for wishing his brother out of the way, for, unless he was aware of the new will which Albrey had drawn up in favour of his niece, Edna Lister, which was scarcely possible seeing that it had only been executed three days prior to the millionaire's death, he was to all intents and purposes the next of kin.

A nudge from Cartwright broke in to John's thoughts and brought him back to his present surroundings.

'Look!' whispered the secretary.

Following the direction of his eyes John saw that a second and rather incongruous figure had just entered through the iron door.

He was a tall man, rather on the thin side, and possessing a slight, scholarly stoop, which the huge, fleecy motor coat he was wearing failed entirely to conceal. A soft, felt hat drawn low over his eyes and a white muffler that was swathed about his chin rendered his face practically invisible. Beneath the coat he was wearing evening dress, for the ends of the immaculately creased trousers fell perfectly over the small, highly polished patent leather shoes and were plainly visible.

The man who had been addressed as Bertram caught sight of the newcomer almost the same instant as John and Harry, and with a word to the other man at the bar with whom he had been talking hastily swallowed his drink and advanced to meet him.

'You're punctual to the minute, Doctor,' John heard him say, and then his voice dropped to so low a tone that the detective strain his ears as he might, couldn't catch the remaining part of the sentence.

The man called 'Doctor' muttered something in reply, and drew his companion over to a vacant table on the opposite side of the room, where they became at once engrossed in earnest conversation. They were too far away for there to be a possible hope of John catching anything of what they said and it was fairly obvious that the later arrival was giving the man with the broken nose some kind of instructions, for he appeared to be doing all the talking, while his companion merely interjected a word here and there, accompanied by an occasional nod of the head to show that he understood.

'It's essential,' said John softly, that we should try and learn what they are talking about. I'm going to try and get nearer to them.'

He drained the remainder of his glass while Cartwright apparently did the same, although in reality with a quick dexterous twist of his wrist he shot its contents under the table. With the glass still in his hand John rose to his feet and made his way over to the bar, the secretary following suit. He tapped with the bottom of the glass on the rough topped table to attract attention.

'Now then, come on,' he growled surlily to Cartwright. 'I ain't goin' to pay for your bloomin' drinks all the evening. It's 'igh time you did a bit of parkerin' up.'

'All right, give us a chance,' answered Harry in an aggrieved tone, and flinging a coin to the barman he ordered, 'Same again, Cully.'

'I ain't goin' to sit at that blinkin' table any longer,' continued John loudly while the drinks were being served. 'There's a draught there enough to cut your 'ead off.'

'Keep yer 'air on,' growled Cartwright. 'What yer goin' to do, stop 'ere?'

John shook his head.

'Not bloomin' likely,' he answered. 'We might as well sit in comfort. There's an empty place over there. See where I mean.' He jerked his thumb in the direction of a table that had just been vacated, within a yard of that occupied by the man called Bertram and his companion.

'All right. Come on then,' said Harry, grabbing his glass. 'Let's get there before someone else pinches it,' and with the rolling gait that is peculiar to the character he was impersonating he made his way over to the table John had indicated.

The two men were still earnestly talking when they seated themselves noisily, a little behind them, and they appeared to be deeply interested in what they were discussing, for they didn't even look up.

'We don't seem to have improved matters much,' whispered Harry, a few seconds later, after he had vainly strained his ears to catch what was being said. 'I'm hanged if I can make out a word.'

'Neither can I,' said John below his breath. 'They're speaking much too softly, but we've got to try somehow. It's too good a chance to be missed.'

He leaned back in his chair, racking his

brain to think of some means that would enable him to overhear what was passing between the man with the broken nose and his companion. Behind the table at which the two were sitting was a thin, unpainted iron pillar, rising to the roof and supporting the central girder that crossed beneath the skylight. It was so close that it almost touched the back of the chair occupied by the man called Bertram. As John noted it a sudden idea flashed through his brain and he leaned forward towards Cartwright.

'I've got it,' he muttered. 'Pretend to quarrel with me and after a minute or two I'll get up in a huff and go and lean against that pillar. See the idea?'

The secretary nodded, and there followed as perfect a piece of acting as had ever been witnessed.

Cartwright began to grumble, complaining that he was getting fed up and that the evening was slow and that he wanted to go somewhere where it was more lively. John grunted replies; and then, as though suddenly losing his temper, he rose unsteadily to his feet and in a raucous, throaty voice commenced to hurl a torrent of abuse at Cartwright's head, swaying slightly as if under the influence of drink. Harry, raising his voice also replied in the same tone, and at last John banged his fist on the table, making the two glasses jump.

'Well then,' he roared, 'you can spend the rest of the bloomin' evening on your own. I've 'ad enough of yer.'

Picking up his glass he swallowed the contents at a gulp and moved unsteadily over to the iron pillar, muttering all the while below his breath. Leaning solidly up against the support and every now and again looking round and glaring at Cartwright he searched in the pockets of his greasy clothes and presently found a packet of cheap cigarettes. After several abortive attempts he succeeded in lighting one of these and commenced to smoke, glowering savagely at the floor.

The scene had aroused very little interest, for it was one that was only too familiar to the habitués of the 'Hole in the Wall'. Many quarrels had taken place in that den of iniquity, and not all of them had ended so peacefully. The old wharf that lay at the back could have told stories of silent and grim burdens that had been carried along its rotting planking and confined furtively under cover of darkness to the river, to form later another mystery for the Thames Police to solve. Beyond a momentary stoppage of the general buzz of conversation at the first high words no notice had been taken. The man with the broken nose had glanced up for a second, but on seeing what was taking place merely shrugged his shoulders, said something with a laugh to his companion and immediately resumed his interrupted conversation.

John was now directly behind him, and listening intently managed to catch above the din that was going on around him a word here and there of what was being said. The man whom Bertram had addressed as 'Doctor' was speaking.

'Everything is going well . . . In a week . . . I shall . . . To strike . . . We could start before if we had . . . '

He couldn't hear the rest of the sentence because the man's voice dropped, but he was able to make out part of Bertram's reply:

'How much . . . ' He missed the rest, and then he distinctly heard the words: ' . . . 'Purple Plague'.'

He suppressed a start, and a wave of excitement ran through him. So they were discussing the mysterious disease. He strained his ears to their utmost, hoping that he might learn something further that would tend to confirm his previous astounding theory that the malady was the result of a human agency after all!

He was certain in his own mind that the man called Bertram was the man he was seeking and that it had been his hand that had stabbed James Albrey. It was quite conceivable, therefore, to suppose that the man Bertram had met by appointment at the 'Hole in the Wall' was also mixed up in the affair. The question was, who was he? A sudden thought occurred to him. Could this be the stranger who had called to see Albrey earlier on the same evening he had met his death, the man who had sent in the note contained in the peculiar, oilskin-lined envelope, and whom Wilby, the butler, had heard quarrelling with his master? John believed that he had hit upon the truth. It was quite possible, even probable but if he was the same how did he fit into the scheme of things? If the man addressed as Bertram was really Albrey's younger brother still alive, and John was fairly certain that he was, the motive for the stabbing of the millionaire was obvious, for, knowing nothing of the later will, drawn up in favour of Edna Lister, by Cranston, he would naturally suppose that being next of kin he was the heir to the old man's fortune. The other man's presence, however, was not so easily accounted for. For what reason had he visited Albrey, and was he the person responsible for the outbreak of the 'Purple Plague'?

John had not time for further thought, the two men were again talking earnestly, and, forgetting in his excitement his usual caution, John leaned forward listening intently. 'All the experiments so far had been satisfactory,' the man called 'Doctor' was saying, 'and we have succeeded in . . . '

John heard no more for suddenly a hand grasped him roughly by the shoulder and jerked him back.

'Here,' demanded a husky voice in his ear, 'what's your little game, eh?'

The detective swung round and found himself gazing into the face of a tall, flashily-dressed man, with a large hooked nose, who was gazing at him suspiciously. It was the same man who had greeted Bertram on his arrival, and asked him to have a drink at the bar.

'Take yer 'ands off me,' growled John truculently, 'or I'll knock yer bloomin' jaw in. What the blazes do yer mean?'

'You're spying,' said the man who had accosted him, still keeping a grip on the detective's shoulder. 'Who are you? I haven't seen you here before.'

'I ain't spyin,' answered John. 'What yer talkin' abart? S'ppose I can lean up against this pillar without askin' you, can't I? Don't own the blinkn' place do yer?'

For a second the man regarded him

steadily and then slowly his hold on John's shoulder relaxed, and the detective drew a breath of relief. But he was premature, for the next moment his captor leaned forward, his left hand shot out and jerked the greasy cap violently from the other's head. In doing so he disarranged the wig John was wearing, so that his own hair became visible underneath.

With a shout of triumph the man tore the wig completely off.

'I knew you were a cursed busy,' he yelled. 'Look out all of you, there's a 'tec' among us.'

For a second there was a sudden hush, and then a babel of excited oaths and shouts broke out and in a moment the place was in an uproar. The man who had first given the alarm flung himself upon John, but with a swift uppercut the detective caught him on the point of the jaw. He collapsed into the arms of his companions who were crowding round, bearing several of them to the ground with him.

Cartwright had sprung to his feet at the

first sign of alarm, and during the brief respite that followed John's action, managed to force his way through the gathering throng to his employer's side.

'We'll have to make a fight for it,' muttered John, his face beneath the make-up drawn and tense. 'We can expect no mercy from this scum if we go under. Keep close to me.'

He had scarcely finished speaking when the rush followed and almost immediately John and Cartwright were surrounded, the centre of a sea of vicious, hate-distorted faces. So confident were they that it would be easy to overcome the two that they rushed in recklessly, and this was their undoing. With his back to the iron pillar, which afforded some protection from behind, John faced the onslaught coolly. His huge arms shot back and forth like steel pistol rods, and every blow he struck reached its objective. He knew that they were fighting for their lives and he put every atom of science, every trick in the art of self-defence and attack that he had learned under the training of one of the best professional boxers going.

Cartwright, who was not slow to follow his employer's lead, added his quota. Holding a chair by the back he swung it about him, smashing it down with all his force on the heads that swayed and struggled around him.

John had managed to clear a space by sheer force of muscle when suddenly a huge black man sprang at him with murder in his drunken eyes and an open razor in his hand. John's right shot out with the force of a battering ram, but the fellow dodged aside and the blow missed. Swift as lightning, however, his left followed it up and caught the man with a half-arm jab full on the jaw. With a sound like a mallet striking wood the man went down with a groan, half his teeth broken. By this time some of the others had recovered and at the fall of their comrade four of them hurled themselves at John, mouthing horrible curses that sounded like the snarls of wild beasts. The foremost went reeling back from a second blow from John's fist that went straight for the solar-plexus, and put him out of the fight for good, but the other three were on him before he could hit again. One of his attackers had drawn an ugly-looking knife that glinted in the electric light and as he raised it to plunge at John's throat Blackmore thought the end had come, but he had forgotten Cartwright.

The secretary had seen what was happening and smashing his way through the struggling knot of hate-mad roughs that hemmed him in he hurled the chair at the fellow's wrist. It went straight for its mark and with a yell the man dropped the knife, his arm numbed and useless from the blow. But now the others, following his example, had drawn knives and John realized that it was but a matter of moments before the superior force of numbers told.

He still fought on desperately, as though searching vainly for some means by which they could escape. A knife ripped down his sleeve as he dodged to one side to avoid the savage thrust, and picking up the man who had wielded it used him as a human battering ram to beat down the howling mob that was snapping round him like mad dogs.

An inspiration suddenly came to John. He knew that it was useless to think of escaping by the way they had entered, for the iron door was locked and could only be opened from the outside, but the skylight offered a chance — if they could only reach it.

He hurled the shrieking wretch he had been using as a shield into the midst of the yelling, cursing mass of humanity that was seething round them. The foremost of his attackers were bowled over like ninepins and the result gave him a second's respite and in that second he acted. In the wall close behind him was a glass-fronted fuse-box that he had noted previously. Gripping Cartwright by the arm he suddenly whipped his automatic pistol from his pocket and fired four shots into the box. There came a shatter of glass and in an instant the place was plunged in darkness.

As John had reckoned, the fuse controlled the single bunch of lights that illumined the room.

'Quick!' he whispered to his secretary.

'Swarm up the pillar and make your way to the skylight. It's our only chance!'

Harry was swift to act on his employer's instructions. Grasping the smooth iron support he started to make his ascent, hand over hand.

With the sudden darkness pandemonium had broken out and above it could be heard a harsh voice shouting instructions.

'Get a light somebody, and guard the door.'

John smiled grimly to himself as he pocketed his pistol and commenced to follow Cartwright up the pillar. If they could reach the skylight before they were discovered escape was practically certain. In the darkness it was impossible for their foes to do anything, for they couldn't see who they were fighting with and might just as easily be tackling one of their own friends.

Up went John and presently his head bumped against the supporting girder. He gripped it and pulled himself up. It was difficult in the darkness to feel his way, but he managed it, and crawled perilously along towards the middle of the roof. He had to move by sense of touch alone for it was pitch darkness and one false step would have sent him hurtling to the floor forty feet below.

Presently a draught of cold air warned him that he was beneath the skylight and looking up he could see the vague outline of it. Cartwright's voice came to his ears.

'I'm through, Mr. Blackmore.'

He felt a hand touch his shoulder. Straightening up cautiously on the girder he gripped the sides of the skylight.

At that moment there came a glimmer of light from below and an electric torch began to sweep about the darkness like a miniature searchlight. Just as John had succeeded in getting his head and shoulders through one of the broken panes the light swept upwards and focused him in its beam. He heard a chorus of excited shouts, followed almost instantly by a crack from a pistol. A bullet hit the iron girder below him with a ping and went whining off at a tangent. A second shot thudded into the roof beside him and then he had pulled himself through and was lying panting beside his secretary on the lead-covered roof.

But there was no time to lose. Now that the yelling mob below had discovered the way by which they had made their escape they would quickly surround the building and try to catch them as they made descent. After a short breather Blackmore scrambled across to the edge and peered down.

There was nothing but a sheer wall to the street below. Not even a water pipe broke its surface and certainly nothing that offered a means of getting down. John looked about him anxiously. The street was little more than an alley and two yards away the coping of a warehouse roof was visible through the thin mist. There was only one thing to do, jump from the roof they were on to the other. It was a hazardous undertaking, but it was the only thing to do, it was impossible to remain where they were.

John explained to Cartwright and the younger man nodded.

'Carry on,' he said. 'You go first.'

John braced himself and with a sudden spring launched himself into space. He landed with a foot to spare and turned to help his secretary. Cartwright followed almost instantly, and the next second they were standing together on the roof of the other building.

It was flat and in the centre projected a raised skylight. Making his way towards this John examined it. It was fastened, but wrapping his scarf round his hand he dealt one of the panes a sharp blow and shattered the glass. When he had cleared away the jagged splinters there was a square hole, large enough for them to drop through.

They dropped into utter darkness and landed a sprawling heap on bare boards. John scrambled to his feet and struck a match. A glance showed him that the building they were in was deserted, and apparently had been empty for a long time for there was dust everywhere. They made their way down a flight of rickety stairs to the lower floor and presently found a window that had been stuffed up with sacking. Removing this they scrambled through and came out into a courtyard.

Two minutes later they were in a street and half-an-hour later were bound for home, bruised and tired, but none the worse for an adventure that had nearly cost them their lives.

6

A Name in a Paper

Despite the fact that it had been in the early hours of the morning before they had sought their bed John was up to time, and when Cartwright entered the study he found his employer had already breakfasted and was preparing to settle down to the perusal of a pile of papers and newspaper cuttings that were spread out on the desk in front of him. John glanced up at his secretary's entrance and smiled.

'Well,' he greeted, 'how do you feel after the excitement of last night?'

'Fine,' replied Harry, warming his hands at the blazing fire for the morning was cold. 'A good healthy fight always does me the world of good. How do you feel?'

'First rate,' said Blackmore, searching in the pocket of his coat for his matches.

'Now, hurry up and get your breakfast, you've got a hard day's work before you.'

'Why? What's the programme?' enquired Cartwright interestedly.

'There are several,' remarked his employer, striking a match and lighting a cigarette. 'Having unfortunately lost our quarry last night, at 'Flimsy' Harris's place the first thing we've got to do is try and get in touch with them again, as soon as possible.'

'How do you propose to do that?' asked Cartwright. 'They're not likely to visit the 'Hole in the Wall' again after what occurred, for they must know that we were after them, and I don't see that we've got the ghost of a clue.'

'As far as the man called 'Bertram' is concerned we haven't,' said John. 'But the other man, his companion, is quite a different matter, and I think that we can easily identify him.'

'How?' asked Cartwright.

'You seem to have forgotten the scrap of paper we found on the path under Albrey's balcony,' replied John. 'If you remember, it ended with the word 'Zat' which I believe to have been part of the name of the sender.'

'Supposing it was,' said the secretary, 'I don't see how that helps us.'

'Think,' said Blackmore quietly. 'Bertram addressed him as Doctor. We are therefore in possession of the fact that the man we are trying to identify is called Doctor Zat . . . something. Now, where is the most likely place to look for further information?'

'By Jove!' cried Harry as a sudden light broke on him. 'What a fool I am. Of course, in the medical directory.'

'Exactly,' said Blackmore, with a smile, 'and if you will hand me that interesting volume we'll look it up and see if it will provide us with the clue we are seeking.'

His secretary crossed to the bookcase, which housed the many books of reference and shortly returned with a fat, red volume that he handed to his employer. John laid it on the desk and rapidly turned the pages until he came to the Z. Harry, who was looking eagerly over his shoulder gave an exclamation of disappointment as he saw that there were over a dozen names beginning Zat.

'I don't see how you're going to pick the one we want out of that lot,' he remarked.

Blackmore's smile broadened and his big finger ran down the pages and stopped opposite a name.

'You didn't suppose for one moment that there would be only one name beginning Z.A.T. did you?' he enquired.

Cartwright didn't reply, he was reading the name at which John's finger pointed: to Doctor Zatouroff. Wyman Chambers, Oxford Street.

'Well, how do you know that's the chap we want?' he demanded.

John laid aside the book and searched among the papers on his desk.

'I don't,' he replied, as he found what he was looking for, a newspaper cutting. 'Now, I'll show you a most peculiar coincidence, if it is a coincidence. Take a look at that!'

He handed the cutting to his secretary. Harry looked at it and saw that it was an account of the first fatality attributed to the 'Purple Plague'. It was not until the end however, that he came across the reason for John's remark, and then he gave such a start of surprise that he almost dropped the cutting. One paragraph read:

'Among the doctors who examined the body were Doctor Julian Zatouroff, a visitor to Bradford. Doctor Zatouroff's hobby is bacteriology, but he can give no reason — '

Cartwright didn't trouble to read further but handed the cutting back to his employer, his eyes shining with excitement. John had acquainted him with his suspicions concerning the mysterious disease on the previous night, after they had returned home, and a brief resumé of his deductions had given rise to those suspicions.

'Do you think,' he asked, 'that this Doctor Zatouroff is at the bottom of this 'Purple Plague' outbreak?'

John nodded.

'I do,' he declared. 'I'm convinced that there is some devilish plot on foot, and that this scoundrel is using the disease for his own ends. What the plot is I haven't the vaguest conception, but I mean to find out.'

'You're basing your theory on rather flimsy evidence, aren't you?' said Cartwright.

'I'm basing it on the evidence of my own common sense,' retorted John. 'James Albrey was in perfect health, according to the statement of his butler, until after someone, a stranger, had called and sent him a note. After that he complained of feeling dizzy and unwell. The note, we discover, was contained in an envelope lined with thin oilskin that rendered it airtight. It was an envelope which had clearly been made for some special purpose. On examining the hands of the dead man I found that the inside of the thumbs and first fingers of both hands were curiously swollen and discoloured, and, in the exact places which naturally come in contact with the sheet of note paper if he had been holding it in his hands to read. Added to this, on no other part of the hands was there a single mark of any kind. Taken in conjunction with the envelope and the fact that the note itself had been carefully removed by the man who had sent it the inference is obvious. I have made several enquiries and as a result I have learned that James Albrey remained in the house all day and nothing could have come in contact with him to infect him with the 'Purple Plague' — except the contents of that envelope.'

'Sounds fairly convincing when you put it like that,' said Cartwright. 'What do you think then is the cause of the disease? Some kind of unknown poison?'

'That is impossible to say,' answered Blackmore, shrugging his shoulders. 'I don't see myself how it can actually be some kind of poison for in the tests that the doctors have already made they have discovered the presence of certain bacilli to which they are unable to give a name. No, I am inclined myself to the belief that it is some new germ that Zatouroff has discovered — you see, the paper says that his hobby is bacteriology, and I should say that it is only virulent while kept unexposed to the air, and that exposure to the air destroys it.'

'That would account for the oilskin

envelope,' said Cartwright, thoughtfully.

'Yes,' replied his employer, lighting a fresh cigarette. 'And it would also account for the fact that as far as we know the 'Purple Plague' is not infectious in a general way. It is probably only infectious during the first few minutes of the disease.'

'Do you think the other deaths, prior to Albrey's, were part of the plot?' asked Harry.

'I can't say,' said John shaking his head. 'That, I'll admit, is puzzling me considerably. They were so far apart and amongst such different classes of people it seems almost impossible to reconcile them to any direct plan.'

'What puzzles me most,' said Cartwright, 'is why Albrey should have been stabbed. If your theory is correct regarding the 'Purple Plague' and if Doctor Zatouroff is the man who sent in the note impregnated with the disease, why did his accomplice, Bertram — and they must be in it together seeing that they met in the 'Hole in the Wall' — go to the trouble and risk of stabbing the man, when he knew that he was already dying from the 'Plague'?'

'Did he know?' asked Blackmore, looking curiously at his secretary.

'He must have known,' exclaimed Harry.

'Not necessarily,' answered the detective cryptically, and changed the subject. 'The question is what motive had Zatouroff — always supposing that we're right and he was the man — for inoculating Albrey with the disease. When that is discovered the rest will be clear. It is certain that in some way or other he was acquainted with the millionaire, an acquaintance that, to judge from what Wilby says, was intimate enough for him to gain an interview immediately on sending in the note although he had never visited Albrey before, and also to try and extort money, as witness the words which the butler heard as he passed by the study door. But what reason could he have for killing him?' John's forehead was puckered in a thoughtful frown. 'We know that the other man, Bertram, had an excellent reason for desiring Albrey's death, for by it he believed he stood to gain a fortune.'

'If he is really Albrey's younger brother,' said Cartwright. 'There's always the possibility that the name is only a coincidence.'

The detective pursed his lips.

'That's true,' he agreed, 'But the coincidence would be rather an extraordinary one, especially as we know that he was the man who stabbed the millionaire, and unless he was Bertram Albrey he could have had no motive for doing so. However, that point will be cleared up one way or the other in a day or so. I have already dispatched a cable to an agent of mine in Montreal asking him to enquire carefully into the circumstances of Bertram Albrey's death, three years ago, and let me have the result of his investigations.'

'But,' persisted Cartwright, 'supposing it does turn out to be Bertram Albrey, that wouldn't account for Zatouroff's connection with the affair and his motive for calling on Albrey and infecting him with the 'Purple Plague'.'

'No, it wouldn't,' replied John quietly.

'But I've an idea at the back of my mind, that would.'

'What is it?' asked the secretary eagerly.

'Never mind for the moment,' said his employer. 'It's too hazy yet to talk about. By Jove!' he added, as the clock chimed the hour. 'It's ten o'clock! We've been talking for over an hour. Hurry up and have your breakfast and then get into your street hawker's disguise, there's a little job of shadowing I want you to do.'

'Who?' asked Harry. 'Zatouroff?'

But to his surprise his employer shook his head.

'No,' he replied. 'At the moment we know where to find Zatouroff if we want him, and I can manage him myself. I want you to shadow that girl, Edna Lister. For the moment Bertram Albrey learns of the existence of that will leaving her his brother's fortune, her life is going to be in the gravest possible danger!'

7

A Midnight Visit

About half way up Oxford Street on the left hand side going from Tottenham Court Road towards Regent Street is a large block of mansion flats.

The flats themselves are invisible from the street for they lie in a square court-yard behind several imposing shops, and are approached through a wrought-iron archway that bears the name 'Wyman Chambers' in ornate gilt letters over its portico.

The chambers had originally been erected by a wealthy philanthropist to provide small model flats for the professional classes who needed a limited accommodation and a good address at a moderate rental.

Like many philanthropists, however, the owner had wearied of his hobby and had sold the block to a syndicate, whose management, if lacking philanthropy, was certainly businesslike and decidedly profitable to themselves. They had turned out all — in their estimation — undesirable tenants and let the flats at a high rental to anyone whose bank balance proclaimed them to be respectable and an acquisition to the chambers.

In a large and comfortably-furnished room in one of the biggest and most expensive of the ground floor flats, a man sat before a littered writing table intently studying a mass of documents that lay on the blotting pad in front of him.

A green-shaded reading lamp that stood at his elbow was the only illumination the room boasted, and the white rays, escaping from under the silken shade, fell full upon his face as he bent forward over his papers.

It was a cruel face, and, as he crouched in his chair, was reminiscent of a bird of prey, poised ready to strike. Below a high forehead, from which the hair, iron grey in colour, had receded at the temples, a thin aquiline nose jutted out aggressively. The sallow cheeks were thin and sunken at the sides of the mouth so that the cheekbones stood out, forming hollows for the piercing eyes that gazed from under hairless brows. A repellent face, and yet a face in whose very ugliness lay character and a certain vague attraction, much the same fascination as is to be found in some species of snakes.

Doctor Zatouroff had long since dealt with his last surgery patient and was engaged in work of quite a different nature. Could some of the people who swore by him as a doctor have been able to gaze into the depths of that evil brain and read the thoughts that were seething there they would have received a rude shock.

For over an hour he sat motionless, moving only to lay aside a page as he finished reading it or to make a brief note in the margin with the gold pencil that he held in one claw-like hand. He appeared to be checking some typewritten list for against certain names he drew a circle.

Presently he finished the last of the pile of papers that lay in front of him, and with a sigh of relief sat back in his chair and stretching out a hand helped himself to a cigarette from a gold box at his side.

He had scarcely exhaled two puffs of the fragrant smoke when a muffled bell broke the silence of the room. Three times it whirred softly and laying the cigarette carefully in an ashtray Doctor Zatouroff rose from the table and crossing the room passed out into the darkened hall.

Opening the front door he saw a figure silhouetted against the light in the vestibule.

'Come in,' he said briefly, and held the door open wider.

The man slipped into the hall, and the doctor closed the door and carefully bolted it behind him. Doctor Zatouroff led the way back into the room he had just vacated and motioned his visitor to a chair.

'Well, Mitchell,' he remarked, in a soft, sibilant voice that closely resembled the hiss of some venomous serpent. 'Is everything progressing favourably?'

His visitor inclined his head.

'Excellently, Doctor,' he replied. 'The

last culture will be complete in three days. When do we make a start?'

'Next week,' said the doctor. 'I want to finish up at the Dartford factory as soon as possible. The rest of the scheme will be carried on from the other place. You saw that the pamphlets were sent there?'

'Yes,' replied Mitchell. 'And the envelopes too.'

'Good,' said Zatouroff. 'I have just finished checking the lists of names. Mason had put in several that were quite impossible. Against these I have pencilled a circle.'

'What shall I do about the workers?' enquired Mitchell. 'The factory can be closed almost at once if necessary.'

Zatouroff snapped his fingers.

'Send them back to the gutter where we found them,' he answered. 'We've no further use for them.'

'Don't you think it will be rather risky?' said Mitchell, dubiously. 'They may talk . . . '

'Nonsense,' grated the doctor. 'Half of them are under the influence of dope, and the others dare not talk for fear of their own skins. I took a lot of trouble in picking those men, Mitchell, when I first conceived the scheme, and although I collected around me some of the cleverest chemists in the world I took care to safeguard myself. All of them are either drug takers, drunkards, or have committed some act against the laws of this country which will prevent them going within a mile of the police. There's nothing to fear from them. Besides, in two weeks' time we shall have scooped our pool and be out of the country.'

'It seems too easy,' said Mitchell, after a short silence. 'Are you sure that you're not trusting too much to luck?'

Doctor Zatouroff looked up, and into his deep-set eyes there shone for a moment an evil glint.

'I have not taken luck into consideration at all,' he replied. 'Everything has been worked out to the last detail. There is no risk of failure. What's made you scared all of a sudden?'

'What about the detective who was at the 'Hole in the Wall' last night?' asked Mitchell deliberately. 'John Blackmore's a clever man and — '

Zatouroff leaned back in his chair with a short laugh.

'He may be,' he retorted. 'But he knows nothing. It is impossible that he can have guessed the truth. We've nothing to fear. Nothing. The only thing that is troubling me is lack of money. It is going to cost a considerable amount to carry out the scheme, and I've already spent every penny I possess in my experiments.'

'You'll have to find a certain amount to pay the men before I can shut down the factory,' said Mitchell. 'I came about that tonight. They weren't paid last week, and some of them are getting restive.'

The doctor's brows met in a frown.

'You will have to put them off with some excuse for a day or two,' he replied. 'By that time I hope to be in a position to raise a considerable sum.'

'Very well, then,' said Mitchell. 'I'll do my best.' He rose to his feet. 'I'll be getting back now, Doctor. I don't like being away from the factory too long.'

'Isn't Bertram there?' asked Zatouroff accompanying his visitor to the door.

The man shook his head.

'No,' he said. 'He left just before I did. Said he'd got some important business to attend to, though I can't see what it can be at this hour of the night. He seemed in a bad temper over something, too. Mason's in charge at the moment, but you can't trust him. He's all right as long as he leaves the drink alone, but you never know when he's going to break out. Is there anything further, Doctor?'

'No,' said Doctor Zatouroff; unbolting and opening the front door. 'If there should be any reason for changing the plans I'll let you know. In any case I shall be down at the factory tomorrow night.'

Mitchell nodded and bade him good night, and after he had gone Zatouroff carefully shut and re-bolted the door and returned to his sitting room. He glanced at the clock and saw that it was nearly half-past-twelve and for some time he stood by the fireplace and stared thoughtfully at the dying embers in the grate.

Then rousing himself from his reverie he crossed the room to a door overhung with a heavy curtain. The room beyond was evidently the doctor's bedroom and switching on the light he went over to a large wardrobe and selected from it a dark tweed suit.

Flinging it on the bed he rapidly divested himself of the dinner suit he was wearing, and donned the other in its stead. Returning to the sitting room he opened a door in the writing table and took out a small, black leather roll that closely resembled a motorist's kit of tools, and slipped it into his hip pocket together with a wicked-looking automatic pistol and an electric torch.

He stood for a moment thoughtfully, and then switching out the light went out into the hall. Putting on a dark overcoat that reached nearly to his heels and pulling a soft cap down over his eyes he wound a muffler about his throat and chin and opening the front door slipped noiselessly out, closing it softly behind him.

He paused for a moment in the vestibule, looking round him, but there was no one about, and walking swiftly across the courtyard Zatouroff passed under the iron archway into Oxford Street.

There were many people in the brilliantly-lighted thoroughfare, for the most part amusement seekers hurrying to catch last buses and trains, and as he strode hurriedly along he attracted little notice.

At Tottenham Court Road he was fortunate enough to catch a bus going City-wards and boarding it he mounted to the top. At the end of the Kingsway he got down. Crossing the road he entered a dark and narrow alley by the side of the Holborn Empire and presently emerged in the broad square of Lincoln's Inn. At this hour of the night it was deserted and Doctor Zatouroff, hurrying along to the left, paused at the end before an old Queen Anne house that stood shoulder to shoulder with other mansions of the same period. A large brass plate of the lintel of the door bore on black letters, 'Edward Cranston, Solicitor'.

Doctor Zatouroff stopped opposite this and glanced to right and left. Everything was quiet and there was not a living thing in sight.

Swiftly and noiselessly he ascended the flight of worn stone steps to the front door. His hand searched in his pocket and then for a few minutes he worked swiftly in the shadow of the portico.

Presently there came a slight creak, followed by a little splintering crash, and then the door opened under pressure of his shoulder. He slipped across the threshold into the narrow and pitch-dark hall, shutting the door softly behind him. No one had seen him enter and he knew that the building was entirely deserted, being given over to offices.

A light winked in the blackness, showed again and went out. Zatouroff had produced his electric torch and in that momentary gleam the rays had shown him a door on his right, marked private. He paused, and before going any further took the precaution of fixing the scarf he was wearing so that its folds concealed the lower part of his face. It was not that he expected to find anyone in the building, for he believed that he had the place to himself, it was just that he was prepared for all eventualities, and if he could help it Zatouroff never took any risks.

He switched on the torch again and approached the door. To his surprise it was unlocked and under the touch of his hand it slowly opened!

Noiselessly he stepped across the threshold. The round white ray of his flashlight cut a filmy path through the darkness and he saw that he was in a sort of outer office.

Then suddenly he stopped, and hurriedly switched out the light of the torch. From somewhere had come to his ears a faint sound. The rustle of papers!

Zatouroff stood motionless, his body bent slightly forward, his muscles rigid and tense, listening with straining ears.

There was someone else in the building! Who could it be? His eyes peering intently into the darkness ahead made out a faint glimmer of light. It came round the edge of a door on the opposite side of the room. The door, thought Zatouroff, led probably into Edward

Cranston's private office, and the some-one, whoever it was, was in there.

The rustling sound had ceased and was followed by the faint rattle of metal on metal.

Zatouroff crept silent forward towards the faint ribbon of light. Halfway a loose board creaked under his weight, and he paused, holding his breath, for fear the sound had betrayed his presence to the unknown person in the room beyond. But apparently whoever it was there had heard nothing, for the sound of papers being moved softly again came to his ears.

He smiled grimly to himself. The intruder was evidently searching for something. But who was it? Could it be Edward Cranston who had come late to his office for something he had forgotten and wished to take home? But this thought he dismissed almost before it came to his mind. Cranston would hardly be likely to work by that faint glimmer, he would have switched on the ordinary electric light. It must be someone, who, like himself, had no right there at all — a burglar.

The doctor's hand slipped beneath his coat and his fingers closed round the butt of the automatic pistol he carried in his hip pocket. Whoever it was, it was going to be unlucky for them that they had chosen the same time as he, for he had not the slightest intention of allowing this unexpected presence to interfere with his own plans.

He had reached the door now, and cautiously leaning forward peered through the small space between its edge and the frame. The room was obviously, as he had thought, Edward Cranston's private office, and the faint light came from an electric torch that had been laid on the top of the large roll-top desk that occupied the centre of the apartment.

The desk was open and bending over it with his back to the door was the figure of a man!

He was dressed in a long coat and appeared to be deeply engrossed in examining the papers, which he had taken from a black japanned deed box that stood beside the torch.

Zatouroff noiselessly pushed open the

door wider and covered the other with his automatic.

'Hands up!' he ordered crisply, and the man, with a startled exclamation, straightened up from his stooping position over the desk and swung round. As he did so the light from the torch fell full on his face.

The doctor almost dropped the pistol in his surprise as he recognized the intruder. It was the man called 'Bertram'!

Without further hesitation the doctor advanced into the office.

'It's all right,' he said coolly, pulling the muffler from his face. 'You needn't get scared. I had no idea it was you.'

The man started as he heard the voice.

'Good Heavens! You!' he gasped. 'What on earth are you doing here?'

Doctor Zatouroff dropped the pistol into his pocket and crossing to the other's side rested his elbow on the top of the desk.

'That remark also applies to you,' he said, and then he caught sight of some white lettering on the side of the deed box, the contents of which Bertram had evidently been examining.

His eyes narrowed as he made out the name.

'What has Albrey got to do with you?' he asked sharply, pointing at the box.

Bertram hesitated.

'Come on,' said the doctor impatiently. 'There appears to be a slight mystery here that requires clearing up. What are you doing here examining James Albrey's private papers?'

'He was my brother,' answered Bertram.

Zatouroff gave a start.

'You — you are Bertram Albrey?' he demanded, and the other nodded. The doctor's brows met in a frown. 'I see,' he said softly, and nodded his head slowly. 'I was a fool not to have guessed it before. So you weren't killed in Montreal after all?'

'No,' replied Bertram. 'The man who was killed was very like me. I was in a bit of a hole at the time and I saw in it a good chance to get out, so I got some friends of mine to identify the dead man as myself.'

'I see,' said the doctor again. 'So it was

you who killed Albrey.'

'It was I who stabbed him,' said Bertram deliberately, 'and at the time I believed I had killed him — until I read the papers,' he added.

'What difference did reading the papers make?' enquired Doctor Zatouroff with the suspicion of a sneer in his voice. 'It doesn't alter the fact that it was your hand that struck the blow.'

'But he didn't die as the result of the knife wound,' retorted Bertram. 'He died from the effects of the 'Purple Plague'.'

'I should not be so sure of that if I were you,' said Zatouroff. 'Even the doctors say that is impossible to be certain which killed him.'

'He died from the disease,' persisted Bertram doggedly. 'You know that perfectly well therefore you are responsible for his death, so what's the use of trying to throw the blame on me.'

'I am by no means responsible for Albrey's death,' replied the doctor harshly. 'I am certain that the disease could not have had time to kill him, and therefore if he was alive at the time you stabbed him you are guilty of his death.'

'But he would have died in any case,' said Bertram hotly, 'even if I hadn't been there at all.'

'That's quite true,' answered Doctor Zatouroff easily. 'But that doesn't alter the fact that you were there. You killed him!'

'I did not,' retorted Bertram angrily. 'I'm willing to admit that I intended to, but you got there first. I meant to tackle you about the affair the other night in the 'Hole in the Wall' but I couldn't very well without giving myself away. What was your object in inoculating James with the 'Plague'?'

'Because I thought he was the only person who stood between me and a fortune,' replied the doctor. 'It was not until after he had become infected with the disease that he told me in a fit of temper that he had made a will leaving everything to a girl called Edna Lister.'

'But how did you expect to benefit by James's death?' asked Bertram, his brows contracting in a puzzled frown.

'Because,' came the startling reply, 'I

imagined that I was next of kin. I had no idea that you were alive then.'

'Who are you then?' demanded the other, staring at Zatouroff in astonishment.

'I am — or to be more correct I was — Albrey's brother-in-law,' answered the doctor slowly.

Bertram Albrey staggered back against the desk, his eyes staring as if he had suddenly been confronted by a ghost.

'Good Heavens! You — you're the man that married Grace?' he cried huskily.

'I am,' said Zatouroff coolly. 'It's an extraordinary coincidence, isn't it, that we should meet like this, and that we should have been associated together for so long without either being aware of the other's true identity. However, I can assure you that you are not more surprised than Albrey was.'

'Did you tell him who you are,' exclaimed Bertram, recovering from his amazement.

'Certainly,' replied Zatouroff. 'I sent him in a note signed by the name he knew me by. He saw me at once, but he was most offensive — threatened me with all sorts of things and finally told me to clear out.'

'James Albrey always hated you,' said Bertram. 'And I am not surprised after the way you treated Grace.'

'You can cut that out,' snarled the doctor roughly. 'I'm not going to stand for any of that from you. I suppose you are here for the same purpose as I am, the Will?'

Bertram shook his head.

'No,' he answered, to Zatouroff's surprise. 'I knew nothing about the later Will in which James left his money to the girl until you told me. I merely wanted to make sure that no Will existed of which I was not aware before making my claim.'

The doctor looked at him curiously.

'How did you intend to claim?' he asked. 'Surely you realized that the moment you revealed your identity you would have been suspected of the murder?'

'I shouldn't have done so,' said Bertram, 'until after I had got back to Canada. There are plenty of people I know there who would have sworn to the fact that I had never left the country.'

Doctor Zatouroff nodded his head slowly.

'You're cleverer than I thought you were,' he admitted. 'Have you found the Will?'

'No,' answered Bertram. 'I've searched all the boxes containing James's papers and effects but there's not a sign of anything in the nature of a Will. I suppose you wanted to find it and destroy it?'

'Of course,' said Zatouroff. 'That was my original idea, because believing that you were dead I imagined that I should inherit the money.'

'But now, even if the Will was destroyed I should get the money,' said Bertram. 'In law I should come before you.'

'I am perfectly aware of that,' replied Zatouroff. 'But before the Will can be destroyed it has got to be found. You're sure you've overlooked nothing?'

'Certain,' said Bertram emphatically. 'You can go through the papers again with me, but it isn't here.'

Together they bent over the desk and

methodically searched through the contents of a dozen or more black deed boxes, each bearing the name Albrey in white letters, which Bertram took down from amidst row upon row of others on the shelves that lined two sides of the office. At the end of an hour they gave it up.

'It's not here,' said Zatouroff. 'If it was anywhere it would be among Albrey's effects. Chisholme must either have taken it home with him or lodged it at his bank. In which case we've had all our trouble for nothing.'

'There's only one thing to do,' said Bertram thoughtfully. 'If we can't find the Will we can't destroy it. But,' — he paused for a second — 'there's an alternative which, if it comes off, will have the same effect.'

'What's that?' asked Zatouroff.

'The Girl,' said Bertram, significantly. 'If we could get hold of the girl we might be able to persuade her to sign over the money to one of us!'

Zatouroff's deep-set eyes glared strangely in the dim light.

'That's quite a good idea,' he said. 'She's working as a cashier in Bellbridge's and it should be quite easy to get hold of her one evening as she leaves.'

'Take her to the Dartford factory,' said Bertram. 'You'll be able to persuade her more easily there if she happens to be at all stubborn.' He ended with a short laugh.

'We'd better get away from here as soon as possible,' said Doctor Zatouroff. 'We've taken a risk as it is in remaining here so long. There's no knowing when some patrolling policeman may discover that the front door latch is broken and if he starts making investigations it's going to be awkward — for him!'

Bertram Albrey picked up the torch from the top of the desk and followed Zatouroff across the outer office into the passage. The doctor opened the street door softly and passed out.

All was quiet in the square, and a moment later the two men slipped swiftly down the steps and walked rapidly away. In Holborn Zatouroff hailed a passing taxi and, bidding his companion jump in, told the driver to take them to Wyman Chambers.

'We can discuss further details at my flat,' said Zatouroff as he settled himself back on the cushions and the cab rolled swiftly Westward.

In less than five minutes they arrived at their destination and letting himself in with his latchkey Zatouroff conducted Bertram into the sitting room.

Far into the night they sat talking, and the first pale streaks of dawn were lighting the Eastern sky when Bertram Albrey finally took his departure.

And the girl who had been the subject of their conversation, at that moment sleeping peacefully scarcely a mile away, little dreamed of the plot that had been hatched against her, or of the peril that awaited her during the next twenty-four hours!

8

Kidnapped!

Edna Lister let herself out of the front door of her tiny flat in Edgware Road and stood for a moment on the step, inhaling deep breaths of the crisp, fresh, morning air appreciatively.

She was a tall, slim girl, with an almost boyish figure, and dressed with that effective neatness which brings the wealthy and the work girl to such a baffling level, in a blue costume of severe cut; a plain white linen coat collar and a small hat which covered but did not hide the fair hair, which against the morning sunlight lent an illusion of a golden nimbus about her head.

Her eyes were blue and deep-set and wise with the wisdom that is found alike in those who have suffered and those who have watched suffering. Her nose was straight but slightly up-tilted, and her lips scarlet and full. It was possible to catalogue every feature of Edna Lister and yet arrive at no satisfactory explanation for her charm, for it did not lie in the clear ivory pallor of her complexion, nor in the trim figure with its promising lines, or in the poise of head or pride of carriage, or in the ready laughter that came to those quiet eyes. In no one particular quality of attraction did she excel. Rather was her charm the charm of the perfect agglomeration of all those characteristics that men find alluring and challenging.

It was barely half-past-eight as she left the flat and, turning towards Oxford Street, started to walk to Bellbridge's. Unless the weather was exceptionally bad she made it a habit to walk to her work every morning and back again at night. Cooped up all day as she was in the big store, she got very little chance for any other form of exercise, and she was sensible enough to know that a certain amount was necessary for her health.

Utterly unaware of the dark plot that had been hatched against her and which was shortly to envelop her in its tentacles, she hastened along the crowded pavement, a fresh and dainty figure in the Autumn sunshine.

A thoughtful frown drew her delicate brows together as her mind reverted to the subject of James Albrey's death. The discovery and the part she had played in it had been a great shock to the girl, and the picture of the room with the dead man sprawling over the desk lingered, ever present, in her memory.

Over and over again she wondered what could have been Albrey's reason for writing to her and offering her the situation as his secretary. It seemed so extraordinary that he should have picked on her, a girl who, as far as she knew, he had never seen in his life, and make her an offer of a position that must have carried with it a certain amount of trust,

She had discussed the matter with her fiancé, Frank Holland, on more than one occasion, but neither of them had been able to come to any satisfactory conclusion. Frank was of the opinion that it was merely an eccentric whim of the old man's, but his argument to substantiate this theory was a trifle vague, for it rested solely on the fact that as Albrey had been a millionaire he must, of a necessity, have been also eccentric. On the lines of the old saying that 'You can't have smoke without fire.'

Neither she nor Frank Holland had been worried much by the police since Inspector Peekers had first questioned them at the house at Staines, and for this she felt grateful, for she wanted to forget that tragic episode in her life as soon as possible. But by the last post on the previous night had come a summons for her to attend the inquest, and it was this that was responsible for the worried frown on her face as she walked swiftly down Oxford Street.

By the time she reached Bellbridge's, however, she had succeeded, by a mental effort, in dispersing the gloom from her mind and as she turned into the staff entrance her face had resumed its normal expression of cheerfulness, which it must be admitted was brought about by the simple process of concentrating her thoughts on the pleasant fact that Frank had promised to meet her that evening and was taking her out to dinner with a dance to follow.

The man who had followed her from her flat to the big store heaved a sigh of relief as he saw the girl's slim figure disappear inside.

Cartwright had spent the whole night in a weary and ceaseless vigil outside the building in which Edna Lister's flat was situated and his hours of duty ended when he had seen her safely into Bellbridge's, and he was free until it was time for her to leave again in the evening. John Blackmore considered that while the girl was in the store she was comparatively safe and the close watch over her movements could be withdrawn.

Harry, therefore, feeling tired and hot-eyed from his sleepless night, began to make his way as quickly as possible back home with visions of a substantial breakfast and several hours of well — earned slumber.

He found his employer in his study when he arrived, engaged in reading the morning papers. The detective looked up with a smile as his secretary entered.

'Feeling tired?' he asked sympathetically. 'Nothing happened?' The last was more a statement than a question.

'Nothing,' said Harry, dropping into an easy chair. 'It's the most unexciting job I've ever struck. I hung about Bellbridge's yesterday evening until the girl came out and then played gooseberry. She was met outside the stores by a young man who I suppose is the fellow she is engaged to. Anyway, he took her to the Corner House in Oxford Street and from there they went across to a picture theatre and spent the rest of the evening holding hands in the dark. It was such a rotten film that I nearly went to sleep, and had to hold my own hand to keep awake. After the show was over he saw her home and that's all.'

Blackmore laughed.

'Never mind,' he said. 'Stick it. I may, of course, be entirely wrong and the girl is possibly in no danger at all, but we mustn't take any chances, and if the people we are up against are going to make any attempt they'll choose some time during the evening or the night. Now cut along and have your breakfast and then get off to bed. I believe it's ready.'

An appetizing odour and the rattle of plates from the next room confirmed Blackmore's statement, and needing no second bidding Harry rose with alacrity.

'I can certainly do with it,' he exclaimed as he went over to the door. 'Hanging about all night in the cold is the finest thing for producing an appetite, I know.'

Blackmore continued his perusal of the papers after his secretary had gone, and having got to the end of the items of news that interested him he thrust them aside and rose. He was in the act of lighting a cigarette when there came a violent ringing at the front door bell.

He heard the maid go along the passage and the door open. For a brief moment a man's voice reached his ears and there was a tap on the door and the maid announced:

'Mr. Edward Cranston.'

The lawyer's face was, if anything,

redder than usual and he appeared considerably agitated.

'I am extremely sorry to worry you so early, Mr. Blackmore,' he exclaimed, as he shook hands with the detective. 'But something has occurred which I feel sure you should know at once.'

Blackmore wheeled forward a chair and motioned to the solicitor to sit down.

'You needn't apologise,' he said when the lawyer was seated. 'I am accustomed to seeing people at all hours of the day and night. What has happened?'

'A most extraordinary thing,' said Cranston. 'I had to go to my office earlier than usual this morning as I have a fairly heavy day and there was some work I wanted to get through beforehand. On my arrival I found that the place had been broken into and my private office turned upside down.'

The detective looked at him sharply. A little gleam had crept into his eyes and his lips tightened into a thin line.

'Was anything stolen?' he asked quickly.

The solicitor shook his head.

'Not as far as I am able to tell at

present,' he replied. 'Of course I have only had time to make a cursory examination, but what has brought me round to you, Mr. Blackmore, is the fact that apparently the only things that have been touched are the deed boxes containing Albrey's private papers. There was nothing among them, however that could have possibly been of any value to anyone. The whole thing is a complete mystery to me.'

'I don't think you have to go very far to seek for an explanation,' said the detective. 'I am not at all surprised. In fact I was rather expecting that something of the sort would happen.'

The lawyer almost jumped out of his chair in astonishment.

'You were expecting it?' he shouted.

'Yes,' answered John, smiling slightly.

'But why?' asked Cranston. 'Why should you be expecting anyone to break into my office? I don't understand!'

'It seems fairly obvious to me,' replied Blackmore. 'You say nothing was touched except Albrey's papers?'

'That's correct,' said the lawyer.

'Then doesn't any motive suggest itself

to your mind?' asked the detective.

Cranston shook his head, his forehead wrinkled in a puzzled frown.

'No,' he answered. 'What exactly do you mean?'

'Unless I am greatly mistaken,' answered John, blowing a cloud of smoke from between his lips, 'the person who was in your office was after the Will. The one you executed, on Albrey's instructions, three days before his death, leaving all his property to his niece Edna Lister.'

'But why should anyone wish to find the Will?' demanded the lawyer.

'In order to destroy it,' answered Blackmore.

Cranston looked more puzzled than ever.

'But what good would it do them?'

'Supposing that Will wasn't in existence,' said the detective, 'who would be likely to benefit by James Albrey's death?'

'Edna Lister,' replied the lawyer promptly.

John Blackmore waved his hand impatiently.

'Leaving the girl out of it for a moment,' he said, 'who then?'

Cranston thought for a moment.

'Why, in that case,' he said slowly, 'the estate would go to the next of kin.'

John nodded.

'You surely don't mean,' began Cranston, excitedly, as he suddenly realized what John was driving at.

'I mean his younger brother, Bertram Albrey,' broke in Blackmore. 'I am convinced that he is still alive, and that it was he who stabbed James Albrey.'

For an instant Edward was too astounded to speak.

'Good Heavens, Mr. Blackmore,' he exclaimed at length. 'I never thought of that for the moment. I suppose you have some good reason for your assertion.'

The detective briefly recounted his adventures at the 'Hole in the Wall', while the lawyer listened with eyes wide with astonishment.

'So you see,' Blackmore continued, 'that unless the name Bertram is merely a coincidence, I have very good grounds for my supposition. I have already cabled to an agent of mine in Montreal asking for the circumstances surrounding his supposed death to be enquired into and I am expecting an answer at any moment. Then we shall know for certain one way or the other.'

'It certainly seems as though you are right,' exclaimed Cranston, 'and of course, if you are, it supplies an obvious motive. I was firmly under the impression that Bertram died three years ago, and so was Albrey.'

'I expect he had some very good reasons for letting every one suppose so,' said Blackmore. 'How was it that the Will was not found among Albrey's effects?'

'It is in my private safe at home,' replied Cranston. 'I took it back there the night after Albrey had signed it. As a matter of fact I intended to bring it to the office today but, to be perfectly candid, I forgot all about it.'

'If you take my advice,' said John, 'you will lodge the Will at your banker's at once, for I hardly think it is safe even at your house. The affair concerning the murder of Albrey is, I believe, only a sideline. I am convinced that there is some big plot on foot that Bertram Albrey is connected with apart from the Will. What the real issue is I have not the least idea at the moment, but I feel certain that it is something entirely fresh in the annals of crime. And don't forget that Albrey wasn't only stabbed, he was also suffering from the disease known as the 'Purple Plague' and it is impossible to tell which really caused his death.'

'But you surely don't believe that the 'Purple Plague' is being wielded by an unscrupulous scoundrel entirely for his own ends?'

'I do,' answered John Blackmore. 'What those ends are, I am not at the moment in a position to state, but I intend to find out before many days have passed.'

Cranston left soon after as he had to meet an important client with whom he had made an appointment, and John spent a busy day making various calls, including a long and protracted interview with a well-known authority on obscure diseases in Harley Street.

From there he went to Holborn and spent some time in close conversation with a man he employed occasionally, and

147

who was the most expert shadower in London.

He arrived back in Baker Street just in time to wake the secretary for his job of keeping Edna Lister under observation. While the young man partook of a hearty tea, Blackmore informed him of Edward Cranston's visit of the morning and the burglary at the solicitor's office.

'It rather tends to bear out your theory,' said Harry when the detective had finished.

'It does,' said his employer, 'and it also renders it necessary to keep a double watch on the girl.'

'Why?' asked Harry with his mouth full.

'Well, if they could have found the Will and destroyed it,' said the detective, 'she would have been fairly safe; but now, unless I am greatly mistaken, having failed in their object Bertram Albrey and his accomplice will direct their attention towards Edna Lister.'

'But what has Doctor Zatouroff got to do with the Will?' asked Cartwright in a puzzled voice.

'A lot!' answered Blackmore cryptically. 'It is not his main object, but he has got quite a lot to do with it, believe me. Now, off you go,' he added. 'And don't forget to be careful.'

Cartwright arrived outside Bellbridge's just as the supports for the big iron shutters, which were drawn over the windows at closing time were being dropped into position, and he had scarcely taken up his stand in front of the big steps when a taxi drew up at the main entrance, and the driver got down from his seat, and crossing the pavement entered.

Harry took little notice of the incident until, after about five minutes, the taxi driver reappeared this time followed by the slim figure of Edna Lister.

The girl stepped into the taxi and the man, closing the door, remounted to his seat behind the wheel.

Instantly Cartwright was on the alert, and as the cab moved off he hailed another that was crawling past and without waiting for it to stop pointed to the cab containing the girl that was disappearing down Oxford Street.

'Follow that cab,' he said to the driver and jumped inside.

$$\star \quad \star \quad \star$$

Edna Lister had barely settled herself on the cushions inside the taxi that had called for her when she was overcome with a feeling of faintness. She struggled against it for a moment or two and tried to tap on the window to attract the driver's attention. The interior of the cab became filled with a strong, sickly odour. The lights outside in the street danced before her eyes, and then became blurred. Her senses swam, she fell back against one corner of the seat, a curtain of intense, velvety blackness seemed suddenly to descend and envelop her and she lost consciousness!

9

On the Trail

Cartwright's taxi gathered speed and was soon running smoothly along in the stream of traffic in the wake of the cab in front.

As he settled himself back among the cushions he wondered if, after all, the girl was merely going to keep an appointment with her fiancé, Frank Holland. In all probability the evening would end up at a theatre or a dance hall and then another long, wearisome vigil outside that flat in Edgware Road.

Harry groaned inwardly as he thought of it. He had long ago outgrown the time when shadowing possessed any fascination, and the prospect of standing at the corner of a street throughout the long hours of the night with a searching wind seeking out every chink in his sartorial armour was anything but exhilarating.

He liked action, something exciting,

something that warmed the blood and sent it coursing through his veins with a thrill. Not dogging the footsteps of a girl who seemed to spend all her available hours of leisure in the company of a good-looking young man. Could the secretary have seen a short way into the future he would have known that the evening was going to be anything but tame in its ending, for before Cartwright again saw the light of another day he was destined to pass through the greatest peril of his life — a peril from which all John Blackmore's skill and resource would be needed to save him!

The taxi in front had reached Trafalgar Square and was heading for Whitehall. At Westminster it turned off into Victoria Street and on past the station.

Cartwright began to wonder if his first surmise was not wrong after all, and by the time they had passed Vauxhall and Kennington Oval his doubts became certainties. Where on earth was the girl going to? It was hardly likely that she was coming all this way to meet Frank Holland.

Straight ahead they went into Camberwell New Road, past Camberwell Green and along Queen's Road, Peckham to New Cross, and still there was no sign of stopping, Harry felt the wave of excitement he had been longing for steal through his veins. He was convinced now that something was wrong. The taxi he was pursuing had increased its speed, and the engine was evidently a good one, for his driver had all his work cut out to keep the cab in sight.

Still on they sped, up Blackheath Hill, across the heath itself, leaving Greenwich Park on the left, and through Kidbrook. Where on earth were they bound for thought Harry? Very shortly they would be out in open country, and still there seemed no chance of the chase nearing its end.

There was not the remotest possibility now that Edna Lister could be making this journey of her own free will, and yet she had certainly got into the cab of her own accord and without any coercion on the part of the driver.

His employer had evidently been right

after all, and this was the move he had expected Zatouroff and Bertram Albrey to make. But what was the destination to be? Where was this long journey going to lead him?

Cartwright hoped that he was on the verge of great discoveries, and his spirits that had been damped by the long hours of unprofitable vigil rose in consequence.

The spirit of adventure was deep set in Cartwright's being, and he was never so happy as when he was on the brink of the unknown, for his imagination was given full play, and he could see great possibilities ahead.

They had passed Shooter's Hill now and were nearing Welling when the secretary felt the cab slow up. The driver twisted round in his seat and opened the door.

'How much further do you want me to go, Guv'nor?' he shouted. 'There must be a pretty good bit on the clock now.'

'That's all right,' cried Harry in reply and hastily pulling a couple of pound notes from his pocket he thrust them into the driver's hand. 'Go on until I tell you to stop and don't lose sight of that taxi!'

'I don't mind,' said the driver, 'but I don't think I've got much more petrol.'

He slammed the door and the cab gathered speed again. The slow up had, however increased the distance between the two cabs, and it took some time before they made up the ground they had lost.

Bexley Heath was passed and left behind, and now they were running along a road lined along each side by hedges, with bleak, flat country beyond. Just before the secretary was thinking that they must be nearing Dartford the cab he was following suddenly turned off into a narrow lane leading, as far as he could see in the darkness, across open country.

Cartwright's taxi was about to swing round in its wake when there came a sudden splutter from their engine followed by a sound like a choking cough and the cab came to a standstill. The driver, opened the door.

'Can't go no further, sir,' he said. 'We've run out of juice!'

Harry didn't wait for any more, he was

out of the taxi in a bound and, flinging another note at the astonished driver went racing after the disappearing tail-light of the cab containing Edna Lister.

Luckily the road was bad and full of potholes and ruts and the cab had, of necessity to slow down. But for this it would have been impossible for him to have kept pace with it; as it was he had to sprint hard to do so.

Suddenly he saw to his left, outlined against the skyline, the black bulk of a large building. The taxi in front turned towards this and began slowing down. At the same time he felt a change in the ground beneath his feet It had become soft and soggy. This, combined with his sense of direction, gave him a clue to his whereabouts and he concluded that he must be somewhere close to the Dartford Marshes.

The cab had stopped in the shadow of the building and Cartwright dropped into a walk. A short distance ahead of him rose a high wall which seemed to surround the building, and keeping close up against this he crept as near the standing cab as he thought was safe. The wall was buttressed at intervals and behind one of these he concealed himself.

The driver of the taxi had descended and approaching the wall knocked on what sounded to the secretary like a wooden door, but the buttress prevented him being able to see. After a pause there came the faint sound of voices and the driver returned to the cab. He was accompanied by another man who stood looking while the driver opened the door and leaned forward into the interior. After a moment he straightened up again and the secretary saw that he was carrying in his arms a limp bundle. He re-crossed with this to the door in the wall.

'The boss is waiting inside,' Harry heard the man who had come out say, and the driver grunted something, in reply which was inaudible to him.

They had both disappeared and Cartwright heard the sound of the door being shut. Instantly he moved forward and presently came upon the wooden door, set flush with the brickwork of the wall. He pushed gently at it and as he had expected, it opened under his hand. He slipped through and shut the door behind him and despite his courage his heart beat a little faster as he did so.

He found himself in a courtyard and to his right were several low, concrete sheds. Immediately in front was a second door leading to the main building. Harry guessed from the look of it that it had been a factory of some description, probably was a factory of the kind that had sprung up like mushrooms and had been as quickly vacated at the end of the War.

A sound reached his ears and he darted for one of the sheds, only just in time, for the next second a figure appeared in the doorway and started to walk hurriedly towards the exit in the wall. It was the driver of the taxi returning, and presently Cartwright heard the sound of the engine being started and a few seconds later the noise of the cab moving off.

He eyed the half open door that led to the factory speculatively. Should he risk it and try and find out what was going on inside? All seemed quiet, and after listening for a moment or two he decided that he would explore further. He crept out from behind the low shed and noiselessly approached the door. Cautiously he stepped across the threshold. Beyond was darkness. Again he paused and listened but not a sound broke the silence.

The blackness was impenetrable and extending his arms at right angles to his body he felt his fingers touch rough brickwork. Apparently he was in a narrow passage, he stepped forward gingerly, feeling his way and after a few steps came up against a solid wall. He soon discovered the cause of this. The passage took a sudden turn to the right. As he negotiated the corner he saw ahead of him a thin line of greenish light. It was low down and the secretary concluded that it came from under a door.

Proceeding with the greatest caution he tiptoed towards the line of light and found that his surmise was correct. It came from under a door that barred the end of the passage. He felt cautiously for the handle hoping that the door would be unlocked. To his surprise it was, and opened as he gently turned the handle and pushed. Instantly there appeared between door and jam a bright vivid green radiance.

He only opened it an inch, he dared not move it any further for he heard now the shuffle of feet and the sound of hollow voices, muffled and indistinguishable. In that light the opening of the door would be seen perhaps by a dozen pairs of eyes for he had no idea how many people were within.

He listened, expecting to hear some words, but beyond the strangled voices and the shuffling of feet crossing the floor he could make out nothing. He pushed the door another inch and glued his eyes to the crack. At this angle he could only see one corner of a wall of what appeared to be a big vault. But presently he saw something that filled him with hope.

Against the wall, thrown by the greenish light, was a high shadow. It was an irregular shadow such as a stack of boxes would make, and it occurred to Cartwright that perhaps beyond his range of vision there was a barricade of packing cases, or some such articles, which hid the door from the rest of the room. He determined to risk it and boldly and rapidly opened the door, stepped through and closed it behind him.

His calculations had been accurate. A stack of crates was piled within two feet of the roof and formed a narrow lobby to anybody entering the way he had come. They were stacked neatly and methodically, leaving an opening at one end between the wall and the last pile of cases.

There was a small slip ladder leaning against the barrier, evidently used by the person whose business it was to keep the stack in order.

Cartwright lifted it noiselessly and planted it against the pile of boxes and then mounted cautiously. And as he looked through the narrow opening between the roof and the topmost line of crates the sight that met his gaze caused him to suppress a gasp of astonishment, and lingered long after in his memory!

10

The Purple Plague Factory

The scene that met Cartwright's eyes was like the tortured nightmare of a maniac. He was gazing at a large broad room, its roof supported by six iron pillars, its walls and floor of stone. The ghastly greenish light came from mercury vapour lamps placed at regular intervals and suspended above three rows of benches that ran the entire length of the room.

At intervals along the benches sat white-clad figures, their faces hidden behind rubber masks and their hands covered with gloves of the same material. In the weird light they looked like demons from some other world. In front of each was a small microscope under a glass shade and a rack filled with shallow porcelain trays.

The eyepieces in the rubber masks were protected with windows of mica, which added to the hideous unreal appearance of the wearers. They all looked alike in this uniform garb, a company of ghosts.

Cartwright's wondering eyes followed the lines of benches and took in every detail. Some of the men were evidently engaged in tests and remained all the time with their eyes glued to the microscope. Others were looking into the shallow porcelain trays and stirring at the contents with long glass rods, one now and again transferring something to a glass slide, which was placed on the stage of the microscope in front of him and carefully examined.

A horrible, indescribable, musty odour permeated the air and made the delicate membranes of Cartwright's nostrils smart and ache.

Only part of the room was visible from his post of observation. What was going on immediately beneath the screen of boxes behind which he was concealed he could only conjecture, but he saw enough to convince him that this was the factory in which Doctor Zatouroff was preparing the deadly germ of death which had been called the 'Purple Plague'.

Some of the workers were filling and sealing test tubes with the contents of the dishes, and these were then passed along to a peculiar machine that occupied the corner of the strange apartment. It was presided over by three of the weird looking workers. These, however, were without the rubber masks, their places being taken by large blue glasses.

The machine itself resembled an enormous X-ray apparatus and underneath the large glass globe was a receptacle into which the tubes were placed.

Every bench held a hundred or more of these tubes, and a blue-flamed gas jet for heating the wax that was used to seal the ends.

The work went on methodically, and only occasionally did one of the workers leave his bench and pass through a door at the far end of the room. Evidently it led to some kind of a canteen, for the secretary heard faintly the rattle of crockery from within.

For nearly half an hour he watched and was beginning to consider what he should do when suddenly he heard a voice from beneath him say:

'If you move I'll blow your head off!'

Cartwright looked down. Under the stepladder stood a man, his eyes glowering and menacing and the ugly black barrel of an automatic pointing straight at Cartwright's head.

'You'd better come down off that ladder,' said the man with a little snarling grin twisting his thin lips. 'The boss'll be interested in you.'

Cartwright saw that there was no help for it, and that it would be suicidal to attempt any resistance. Reluctantly he began to descend from his precarious perch.

'Come on, look slippy,' growled his captor impatiently.

The secretary reached the floor, and with the muzzle of the pistol digging in his back was marched across the narrow gangway between the wall and the pile of boxes to the side of the room beyond, which he had been unable to see from his position on the ladder.

'This way,' said the man, and piloted him towards a low door close beside the wall of packing cases.

He could hear a muffled hum of conversation proceeding from the other side, which ceased abruptly as his captor flung open the door.

'I've got a little surprise for you, Boss,' he cried, pushing the secretary in before him. 'I found this fellow nosing about inside the place.'

The tiny apartment was furnished roughly as an office, and seated at the plain deal table that occupied the centre were three men. They had looked up in surprise at the sudden opening of the door, and Harry instantly recognized two of them. The man called Bertram and the man who had met him at the 'Hole in the Wall'. The other man, who was seated on the edge of the table, was a stranger to him.

Cartwright eyed the central figure of the three steadily. So this man with the cruel, hawk-like face and deep-set, burning eyes was Doctor Zatouroff, whom John Blackmore believed was responsible for the 'Purple Plague' deaths!

For a second they looked at Cartwright and his captor in amazement not unmixed with fear. Zatouroff was the first to speak.

'Where did you find him, Mason?' he asked in his harsh, grating voice.

'Spyin' from the top of a ladder behind the pile of packing cases,' answered Mason, jerking his head towards the door, and leering menacingly at the young man. 'I'd just been along to the store room and caught sight of him as I was coming back.'

Zatouroff turned his hard cold eyes again on Cartwright.

'Who are you?' he demanded harshly. 'What are you doing here?'

Cartwright was silent.

'So you refuse to answer, eh?' went on Zatouroff. 'You are very foolish. I have several methods, my young friend, for opening the lips of the people who refuse to speak.'

The words were quietly spoken, but the

tone in which they were uttered caused a sudden sensation of icy coldness in the region of Harry's heart. A conviction seized him that this man with the high forehead and the thin-lipped mouth was utterly merciless and would stick at nothing to gain his own ends.

'Search him, Mason,' snapped the doctor.

The man obeyed with alacrity. Clumsily his hands ran through the secretary's pockets and brought to light his revolver and torch, which he tossed on to the table.

'Is that all?' asked Zatouroff.

Mason nodded, and then suddenly his eyes glinted and he withdrew from the side pocket of Cartwright's disreputable jacket a dirty and creased envelope.

As his eyes fell on the address he gave a startled cry.

'Good Heavens!' he gasped. 'This is addressed to John Blackmore!'

'John Blackmore!' It was the third man who had echoed the name and his face had suddenly gone white and strained.

'Then this must be that confounded

secretary of his — Cartwright,' broke in Bertram excitedly. 'I wonder if his cursed Boss is anywhere about.'

Doctor Zatouroff's lips tightened until they became such a thin line as to be almost invisible and his eyes glittered with an evil light.

'We had better make sure,' he hissed softly. 'You, Mitchell,' — he glanced at the man at his side — 'you go with Mason and search the whole place thoroughly inside and out. Leave this fellow with us.'

Mitchell nodded and slipped off the edge of the table where he had been seated and crossed over to the door. 'Come on, Mason,' he said. 'Bring your gun with you.'

The two men went out and Cartwright was left alone with Zatouroff and Bertram.

The doctor surveyed him for some time in silence, his long, claw-like hand tapping on the table, then turning to Bertram:

'Take this fellow to the stone room with the iron door,' he said after a pause. 'I'll

169

deal with him myself presently.'

'Well,' demanded Bertram when he returned, 'What are we going to do now? It's unsafe to remain here any longer. Even if that fellow is alone there's no knowing how soon John Blackmore may follow him. We'd better clear out while we've got the chance.'

'I intend to,' replied Zatouroff shortly. 'After all, we've finished with this place anyway and it's only anticipating matters by a few hours. As soon as Mitchell and Mason come back they can get rid of Phelps and Bridgers and the rest of that drink and drug sodden crew.' He shot a contemptuous glance at the door leading into the main building. 'We can collect all the tubes of culture and take them with us to Richmond.'

'Do you think it's safe to go there; what about Blackmore?'

The doctor shrugged his shoulders.

'Blackmore may be remarkably clever,' he sneered, 'but he can't know anything about the place at Richmond. Anyhow, I intend to risk it. Having got so far I am going through with the scheme. I have no intention of giving it up now. Think what it means — millions!' His eyes glittered greedily.

'What about the girl?' asked Bertram.

'We shall take her with us,' replied Zatouroff. 'I think I had better see her. She must have recovered her senses by now.'

He rose and walked to the door.

'And the fellow. What are we going to do with him?' asked Bertram.

Doctor Zatouroff paused and looked back at Bertram.

'He will remain here,' he answered with a sinister smile curling the corners of his cruel mouth. 'He is apparently interested in the 'Purple Plague'. He shall have an opportunity of studying it at close quarters!'

★　★　★

Edna Lister returned to consciousness with a sensation that something was hammering at regular and frequent intervals on the crown of her head, and with every blow she winced.

171

It was some time before she realized that the hammering came from within, and not from without as she had at first supposed.

She opened her eyes and looked about her.

She was lying on a packing case, the top of which had been strewn with straw to make it softer, in a small stone room, little bigger than a cell.

There were no windows, what little light there was, was coming from a candle that burned unsteadily on a small wooden shelf. The ventilation depended on a small skylight on the roof that was protected by rusty iron bars.

In one corner was a sort of earthenware sink from the tarnished tap of which a steady trickle of water flowed.

After lying still for a little while, until she had recovered her senses and overcome a sense of nausea, she sat up and dragged herself to her feet.

The exertion made her head reel and she had to maintain her balance by holding on to the wall, and with great labour and with her head throbbing at every step she managed to make her way to the sink.

Turning on the tap and cupping her hands to catch the stream of water, she slaked her appalling thirst. Then she did what most women would have hesitated to do — she put her head under the cold stream, thankful that she had allowed herself to be shingled. Wringing the water from her hair she stood up.

The pain in her head had diminished and her immediate and most prosaic requirement was a towel.

There was no such article at hand and she had to do the best she could with a totally inadequate handkerchief. She was beginning to feel nearly normal again and glanced at the watch on her wrist. The hands, to her surprise, pointed to half-past-nine!

It had been six o'clock when, in response to the note brought by the taxi driver, she had stepped into the cab outside Bellbridge's. In three and a half hours she had been taken — where?

She sat down on the packing cases and tried to create from her confused thoughts some clear idea of her situation.

Fumbling in her bag she found the note and opening it again read the contents. It was typewritten and ran:

'DEAR EDNA,

'I must see you urgently. Will you meet me at Piccadilly Circus Tube Station. I have sent a cab for you.

'FRANK.'

She realized that it had been a trap, but by whom and for what reason?

The driver of the taxi must have been in it. She remembered the sickly odour that had filled the cab. It must have been a drug of some kind. It seemed equally obvious that she had been kidnapped, but who was responsible, and the motive for the action she could not conceive. It was a complete mystery. Now that the pain in her head had diminished and her senses were getting clearer she began to feel a little frightened. What was this place to which she had been brought?

She rose to her feet again, with the intention of making a more detailed examination of her surroundings. She heard a step outside the door, the sound of a key in the lock, and then a man entered the room.

'Well,' he said, closing the door behind him, 'how do you feel?'

She looked at the high forehead and hawk-like nose, the thin lipped sneering mouth and shivered. Doctor Zatouroff saw the shiver and smiled sardonically.

'You mustn't be afraid,' he said, 'unless you act foolishly, in which case you have everything to fear.'

'Why have you brought me here?' she demanded, her voice trembling in spite of her efforts to keep it steady. 'Who are you?'

'Who I am,' he replied harshly, 'is not important at the moment. Why I have caused you to be brought here is a simple matter to explain. I require your signature to some documents.'

Edna stared at him, wide eyed.

'My signature to documents,' she repeated. 'I don't understand. What documents? Why?'

'Because,' said Zatouroff, 'you are a

very rich woman and I want your money.'

'I — rich!' she replied in amazement 'I think you must have made a mistake. I'm only a shop girl — absolutely penniless.'

Zatouroff laughed, a mirthless chuckle that was not good to hear.

'I never make mistakes,' he answered. 'It may interest you to know that you are the sole heiress of an interesting gentleman named James Albrey!'

'James Albrey!' she gasped. 'The man who was murdered!'

'The man who was killed,' he corrected. 'Murder is a stupid, vulgar word. Yes, you are his heiress. Why he should have left his money to you I can't imagine, but he was always eccentric. I have a document prepared making that money over to me, which you will sign.'

'I will not!' cried the girl.

'Then,' said the doctor significantly, 'you will be sorry, I've told you that no harm will come to you if you are sensible and do as I wish. If you are not sensible, imagine the worst that can happen to you and that will be the least! I will treat you so that you will not think of your

176

experience let alone talk of it!'

There was a cold malignity in his voice that made her shudder. She realised that he meant every word that he said.

'Circumstances have made it necessary,' he continued, 'that I should leave here immediately. You will go with me. I shall return for you in an hour. Think over what I have said, and I should advise you, for your own sake, to be — sensible.'

Without another word he turned and left the little room, totally unaware that the girl he had been threatening and who was now sobbing in her fear of him was his own daughter!

★ ★ ★

Harry Cartwright gazed about him at the long low roofed, narrow stone chamber into which he had been thrust by Zatouroff's confederate, and his thoughts were bitter. Like the veriest tyro he had allowed himself to be caught, entirely through his own over eagerness and lack of caution.

The room he was in proved to him

beyond doubt that the factory was a relic of the War for it had evidently at that period been used for the filling of bombs. The secretary had seen too many such places before to be mistaken. There were no windows, and down one wall ran a broad stone bench. There was no woodwork of any kind, even the door being sheathed with iron.

A single electric light set in the wall and protected by a thick concave of glass lighted the apartment.

Cartwright could hear a muffled sound of movements going on outside and guessed, rightly, that Zatouroff was preparing his departure. He wondered what was going to happen to himself. Was Zatouroff clearing out and leaving him to a slow death by starvation?

He remembered the doctor's words.

'I will deal with him myself presently.'

He remembered also the tone in which they had been uttered, and concluded that Zatouroff had something else in mind. An idea of what it was flashed through his mind and in spite of his courage the blood drained from his face and he felt a sudden sensation of physical sickness. It was too horrible to contemplate, and Harry tried to switch his thoughts in another direction.

What about the girl, Edna Lister? What were they going to do with her?

The time dragged and he was beginning to think that they had already gone and the place was deserted when he heard a faint sound at the door. A second later it opened and Doctor Zatouroff and the man called Bertram entered. They were both clad in heavy overcoats. The doctor surveyed the young man menacingly.

'We are about to depart,' he said, 'but as you appear to have taken such an interest in my affairs I felt that I could not go without giving you a little demonstration of a discovery of myself which is unprecedented in the world of science.'

He held up a small glass tube.

'This tube,' he continued, 'contains the germs of which the newspapers have referred to as the 'Purple Plague'!'

Cartwright guessed what was coming, felt a wave of horror pass over him, but by

179

an effort of will he continued to keep outwardly calm.

'If you have followed the various accounts,' said Doctor Zatouroff, 'of the deaths of the people who have unfortunately had to be sacrificed in the course of my experiments, you will be perfectly cognizant with the symptoms of the disease.' He rotated the deadly tube slowly in his long fingers. 'If anthrax germs are exposed for even a few seconds to the action of ultra-violet rays,' he proceeded, 'they change more or less, but quickly return to their original form. If, however, the action of the rays is continued, the microbe changes into a coccus, and then into a filiform bacillus. This form is stable. The germ is also changed in other respects than mere shape. It has entirely new characteristics. It produces a disease entirely different from that of the anthrax bacillus from which it is derived — a disease causing death within five hours of inoculation!

'I am telling you this' — his voice took on a sinister ring — 'so that as you feel the first sensation of the malady gradually steal over you, you will be aware to some extent of the causes from which they arrive. As far as I am able to judge from my previous experiments it is a perfectly painless death.

'I am afraid I shall have to leave you now but before doing so I propose to smash this tube — the air will become charged with the germs that it contains and for a few minutes after their exposure to the air they are virulent! After that they become harmless. That five minutes, however, will be sufficient for you to have been inoculated with the 'Purple Plague'!'

Zatouroff stepped back towards the door as he finished speaking and raised his hand holding the glass tube.

The full horror of the situation flooded Harry's brain and with a hoarse cry he sprung at Zatouroff. Bertram Albrey, however, stepped between, and, catching the secretary, flung him to the ground.

Cartwright hit the stone floor with a crash that knocked the breath out of him, and, before he could recover, Zatouroff dashed the tube to the floor, where it splintered into a thousand pieces, and slipped through the door with Bertram Albrey banging it to and locking it behind him.

Cartwright was left alone — alone in that germ-infested air, faced with the prospects of a horrible death, and without a chance of escape. Something seemed to snap in his brain. With an inarticulate cry he staggered to his feet and pounded madly on the iron door, clawing and tearing at it until his fingers were bleeding and his nails broken. For a second the ghastliness of his position had rendered him panic-stricken.

And then before him rose the vision of a face, the face of John Blackmore, and Harry, with a supreme effort, strove to regain his self-control.

His employer would never have given way as he was doing. Well, he would strive to emulate him and if he had to die he would at least die game!

He pulled himself together and tried to think. He had at least four hours before the end and at present he felt no ill effects. If only he could in some way communicate with Blackmore . . .

Forcing himself to be calm Cartwright examined the door. It took him only a few minutes to become convinced that escape that way was hopeless. Nothing short of dynamite would open that barrier. What could he do?

He began to walk up and down thinking — thinking . . . He felt that if he stopped for a moment he would lose the grip over his nerves.

How long he continued that ceaseless pacing he never knew, but suddenly, in the midst of his tramping a wave of dizziness swept over him! He staggered and had to clutch at the stone bench for support. The disease was already entering into his system!

The thought spurred Cartwright to a final effort. Was he to die like a rat in a trap without even a last word to his employer and friend. Could he perhaps leave a message. With a shaking hand he felt in his waistcoat pocket for the pencil he always carried. It was still there, Mason had overlooked it in his search.

But now the light was becoming blurred before his eyes and there was a dull hammering in his brain. He must be quick. He staggered to a little heap of rubbish in a corner in search of a scrap of paper on which to write his message. As he bent to turn it over his eyes fell on a little glass panel set flush in the stone wall. It was covered with dust and almost the same colour as its surroundings.

His head was spinning and a strange lethargy was creeping over him so that his limbs felt like lead.

With his handkerchief he wiped the glass and saw, by an effort, for everything was dancing before his eyes, the word 'Fire' in letters that had once been red.

It took the secretary some time to grasp the meaning of this. Of course . . . it was a fire alarm. Harry fought desperately to clear his brain.

Was it still connected with the station?

If so it was a chance of getting a message to Blackmore!

He was so weak that it was only at his third attempt that he managed to smash the glass and pull the small brass handle inside.

His skin felt hot and dry and his blood

seemed to have turned to molten lead in his veins. Great waves of velvety blackness descended on his senses . . .

With his last remaining strength he picked up a dirty scrap of paper and shakily scrawled:

'Dying . . . Purple Plague . . . Phone John Blackmore . . . Cartwright.'

He crawled over to the door, he was past being able to walk, and pushed the paper underneath. He had scarcely done so when the blackness came again and Harry, with a little sigh, rolled over — unconscious!

11

A Race Against Time

John Blackmore rose from his desk with a yawn, and started as he saw that the hands of the clock were pointing to half past eleven.

He had spent the evening clearing up some outstanding business connected with a minor case. It was purely routine work and utterly uninteresting, but it had to be done and the detective was glad that the uncongenial task was finished.

He rose from his seat, stretched himself, lit a cigarette, and then dropping into an easy chair before the fire, he stared at the red coals, allowing his thoughts to return to Zatouroff and the 'Purple Plague'.

Shortly after his secretary had left, Blackmore had received an answer to his cable from Canada, and that answer had confirmed his suspicions that Bertram

Albrey was still alive.

Blackmore's case was now practically complete, and as soon as he could discover the whereabouts of Bertram Albrey — which he hoped to do through Zatouroff — he was ready to lay his evidence before Inspector Peekers, and obtain a warrant for the man's arrest on the charge of stabbing James Albrey.

He could, quite easily, have arrested Zatouroff at once, but he was loath to do so for two reasons. The first being, that by doing so he saw the possibility of destroying his only chance of getting on the track of Bertram Albrey. And the second because he was anxious to discover the mystery of the 'Purple Plague'.

Although he was perfectly certain that it was connected with some stupendous plot, Blackmore was entirely at sea as to what that plot could be. He had devised theory after theory, but each one, on being tested by his keen, analytical brain had revealed a discrepancy, and in the end he had discarded them all.

Nothing could be done now but wait.

The detective possessed a fund of infinite patience, but it was irksome to a man of his energetic nature to have to suffer any period of inaction, but there was no help for it.

A slight hitch had occurred. Earlier in the evening, Burke, the man whom Blackmore had put on to watch Zatouroff, had rung up to say that he had lost track of the doctor.

Zatouroff had left his flat in Wyman Chambers at six o'clock, and Burke had lost him in the crowd at Oxford Circus Tube Station, into which he had turned. Whether Zatouroff was aware or not that he was being followed it was impossible to say. But the fact remained that Burke, one of the most skilful trailers he knew, had lost his quarry.

It did not, however, cause Blackmore any uneasiness, for he felt certain that Zatouroff would eventually return to his flat, and he had instructed Burke to go back to Wyman Chambers, and try and pick up the doctor's trail again, there.

He finished his cigarette and was beginning to think about retiring to bed when suddenly the shrill ringing of the front door bell disturbed the otherwise peaceful silence of the house!

He went out into the hall, switched on the light and unbolting the door opened it. Two men stood on the doorstep and as the light fell on their faces Blackmore recognized with surprise that one was Inspector Peekers. The other was a tall, well built, clean shaven young fellow, of between twenty-five and thirty. 'I'm sorry to disturb you so late,' began Peekers, as Blackmore motioned them to come in, 'but I was hoping that we should catch you up.'

John led the way to his study.

'What is it?' he asked, when his visitors were seated.

'This is Mr. Holland,' said Inspector Peekers, introducing the young man with him. 'You will remember that he was with Miss Lister at the time they made the discovery of James Albrey's death at Staines.'

John looked across at Frank Holland, and saw in the brighter light of the room, that his face was white and drawn, and that his eyes looked haggard with worry. His hands were trembling violently and he looked as if it was only by a tremendous effort of will that he was preventing himself from losing his self-control.

'A most extraordinary thing has happened,' went on the Inspector. 'I happened to be at Scotland Yard in connection with the Albrey Case, when Mr. Holland arrived to say that Miss Lister had disappeared.'

Blackmore started and his eyes glinted strangely. So he had been right in his surmise after all!

'Tell me all about it,' he said briefly.

'It's terrible,' burst out young Mr. Holland, 'I am nearly mad with worry. I had arranged to meet Edna outside Bellbridge's at six. We were going to have something to eat somewhere, and then going on to a dance. But some work in the office detained me and it was half-past before I was able to get there. She was nowhere to be seen, and I thought at first that she had got tired of waiting and had gone home to her flat in Edgware Road.

'I was on the point of leaving and going there in search of her when one of the girls from Bellbridge's whom I know slightly and who is a friend of Edna's, came out. She seemed thoroughly surprised at seeing me, for it appeared that Edna had left early, on receipt of a note which was brought by a taxi driver, asking her to meet me at Piccadilly Circus at once, as it was urgent. She had shown the note to her friend. You can imagine what a horrible shock it was to me, Mr. Blackmore, for I hadn't written any note at all!

'I began to think that there must be some mistake somewhere, but the girl was emphatic and stuck to her story. I thought possibly someone had been playing a joke on Edna and so I went straight up to her flat, thinking that perhaps she had discovered the hoax and gone home. But the place was in darkness and although I knocked and rang several times I could get no answer. I waited there for an hour but there was no sign of Edna and at last I began to get really worried and decided to go to Scotland Yard. I was lucky enough to run into Inspector Peekers and it was he who suggested that we should come round here. What can have happened to Edna? Where can she be?'

He rose to his feet and began to pace restlessly up and down.

'I don't think you need worry so terribly,' said Blackmore kindly. 'My secretary has been watching over Miss Lister for some time, and wherever she is at the moment, I don't suppose he is very far away.'

'But why?' demanded Holland, stopping suddenly in his walk. 'Did you expect this to happen then?'

Blackmore nodded, and the Inspector looked at him in astonishment.

'I did,' he replied. 'Otherwise I should not have considered it necessary to put my secretary on to watch the girl.'

'But where has she gone?' demanded the young man impatiently. 'Who sent the note that was supposed to have come from me and what reason had they — '

Blackmore checked the impetuosity of the outburst with a raised hand.

'You must try to control yourself,

Holland,' he said. 'I know exactly how you feel about the matter, but we can do no good at the moment. Until we hear from Cartwright we are powerless.'

'But what's at the back of it all, Mr. Blackmore?' demanded Inspector Peekers, 'Has it got any connection with Albrey's death?'

'It has every connection,' answered Blackmore grimly, and briefly and tersely he outlined to Peekers and Frank Holland the result of his discoveries.

'Good heavens!' cried the young man, when he had finished. 'Do you mean to say that Edna has been kidnapped by these scoundrels. But why?'

'I'm afraid I can't tell you the reason,' said the detective, for he remembered that Cranston had only told him the contents of the Will under a strict promise of secrecy.

'But can we do nothing?' cried Frank Holland, clenching his fists impotently. 'It is dreadful to have to sit here while she — '

The shrill ringing of the telephone bell broke in upon his words. John Blackmore crossed to the instrument and took down the receiver.

'Hello,' he said, 'hello. Yes, this is John Blackmore speaking.' There was a slight pause, and then Inspector Peekers, who was watching him, saw his face go suddenly grey and haggard, and the hand that held the telephone trembled slightly. 'Near the Dartford Marshes, you say,' the detective continued, and his voice sounded utterly unlike his own. 'All right. I'll be there as soon as possible.' I am starting now. Get a doctor and do everything you can.' He hung up the receiver.

'It's Cartwright,' he said huskily, in answer to the inspector's brief question. 'That inhuman scoundrel Zatouroff has inoculated him with the 'Purple Plague'. He is unconscious now at some factory on the Dartford Marshes. Somehow or other he managed to get in touch with the fire brigade before he went under, and told them to phone through to me. It was the chief who rung up just now.'

'But — ' began Frank Holland.

'We've no time to waste in words,'

snapped the detective. 'It's a matter of life and death, and we've got to act quickly.'

He rushed into the hall and reappeared a second later struggling into a heavy overcoat. He was trying to regain his habitual calm.

There was only one chance, and that was that during the next four hours Blackmore could find Zatouroff and force from him a antidote, if such a thing existed, to the terrible disease.

He hurried out of the flat scarcely conscious whether Inspector Peekers or Holland were following him or not, and ran as hard as he could to the garage round the corner, where the car was kept.

A few seconds later he swung the car out into Holborn and sent it tearing along towards Oxford Street. Crouched over the wheel, his eyes peering straight ahead, his lips set in a hard thin line, the detective drove as he had never driven before.

People turned on the pavements to stare after the great car as it thundered past, shaving motor buses and taxi-cabs by inches. At Marble Arch a policeman tried to stop them but Blackmore, despite the outstretched hand drove on, and the constable had to skip out of the way to avoid the car as it swung on two wheels round into Park Lane.

Inspector Peekers and Frank Holland had to hang desperately to the sides to save themselves being thrown out.

On, on went Blackmore, and to the rhythmic hum of the engine and the swish of the whirring wheels hammered in his brain the words: Would he be in time. Would he be in time. Would he be in time.

They averaged a speed of sixty miles throughout that journey, for Blackmore slowed down only when it was absolutely necessary for their safety.

He handled that high-powered car like a living thing, and the machine behaved splendidly, answering to every touch of the man behind the wheel.

They passed through Bexley Heath at five minutes past one — a record journey, for Blackmore had done the distance from home in less than an hour.

Along the open country road he jammed his foot on the accelerator and let the great car all out. They were bordering on eighty miles an hour, and the car bumped and swayed from side to side, like a leaf blown along in a gale of wind.

Suddenly the blaring headlights glittered on the brass helmet of a fireman standing by the side of the road, and with a grinding of brakes Blackmore brought the great car to a standstill and sprang out.

'My name is Blackmore,' he jerked, gripping the man's arm. 'Was it you who phoned me? Which way do we go?'

'It's just down this path,' said the fireman. 'On the left.'

Blackmore went tearing on almost before the man had finished speaking, and he ran so fast that Inspector Peekers and Frank Holland found it difficult to keep pace with him.

In a short while they came upon a fire engine standing outside a door in the wall of a high building.

Blackmore stopped and looked round.

'Where is my secretary?' he asked as the fireman who had met them came panting up.

'I'll lead the way, sir,' he gasped. 'Follow me.'

'Hurry then,' snapped Blackmore. 'Every minute is precious. Did you get a doctor?'

'Yes, sir,' panted the man as they passed through the door in the wall, and crossing a narrow courtyard they entered the main building. 'He's with the young man now.'

The fireman led the way across a big vault like room, and Blackmore gave a quick glance to right and left at the dismantled benches and the electric machine in one corner.

In a small room on the opposite side they came upon a group of three or four firemen and a man who was bending over something on a rough table.

It was Cartwright!

The secretary's face was deathly white and he lay rigid and still.

'I've done everything I can, Mr. Blackmore,' said the doctor as the detective bent over his secretary, 'but I'm afraid that it wasn't much. I've never experienced a case like this before. I understand that it's the 'Purple Plague'.'

'Will you carry him to my car,' he said to the fireman. 'Make him as comfortable as possible. I suppose there was no one else here when you arrived?'

The Chief of the Fire Brigade shook his head.

'No, sir,' he replied. 'The whole place was deserted. I doubt if it could have been left very long though, because the ashes of a fire in that room are still warm.'

He jerked his head across to a door that stood half open in the right wall of the room beyond.

'What can have happened to Edna,' said Frank Holland brokenly. 'If your secretary is following her she must have been brought here. What have they done with her? Can it be possible that the fiends have also — ' His voice ended in a husky sob.

'I don't think you need fear that,' said Blackmore. 'In fact you needn't worry about her for the moment. If they had intended harming her in any way they would have done it here. The fact that she has been taken with them shows that she is fairly safe, for the time being, anyway.'

He glanced sharply about him as Cartwright was carried gently out in the arms of the fireman.

'What we've got to do, Peekers,' said Blackmore, 'is to try and find some clue as to where Zatouroff and his companions have gone to.' He looked at his watch. 'We've got barely two hours and a half to find him in if my secretary's life is to be saved!'

The Inspector looked dubious.

'I don't see how you're going to do it,' he said in a low voice. 'They may have gone anywhere and — '

But John had already hurried away and was peering into the small room where the Chief of the firemen had said the remains of the fire were. It had evidently been used as an office, and there were signs in plenty to indicate the hurried departure of the occupants. The grate was piled with charred papers and a great heap of torn up bills and invoices littered one corner.

Blackmore crossed to these and rapidly but methodically examined them. But there was nothing there to give him the clue he was seeking.

The charred remains in the fireplace yielded nothing either and it was with a sinking of his heart and a feeling of despair that the detective finally gave it up and stood thoughtfully in the middle of the room pulling irritably at his chin.

A quarter of an hour of the time had already gone by and John began to feel hot and cold. Then suddenly he made a quick dart forward. A tiny speck of white had attracted his attention under the edge of the curved flue of the fireplace.

He pulled it down. It was a half-burned scrap of paper and had evidently been carried there by the draught and stuck.

Blackmore's exclamation as he made out what was written on it brought Inspector Peekers and Frank Holland to his side.

'What is it?' asked the Inspector eagerly.

'It's a clue,' said Blackmore, his eyes gleaming. 'A very faint one but it may lead us to the man we want.'

Peekers looked at the charred paper in

the detective's hand and his forehead wrinkled into a frown.

It was part of a business letter from a firm of estate agents, and ran:

'Geo Leroy, Esq.,
Brixham Mantle Factory,
Dartford.

'DEAR SIR,

'We are in receipt of the cash payment for the purchase of the house — '

The remainder of the letter had perished in the fire!

'I don't see how it helps,' said Peekers. 'It doesn't mention where the house is. It might be anywhere.'

'Yes,' but the estate agent will know,' said John. 'Their name and address is printed on the top: 'Ezra Marlow & Co. Come on, we haven't any time to lose.'

He hurried out of the office and found the doctor.

'Where is the nearest telephone?' he asked. 'Going from here towards London, I mean.'

The doctor thought for a moment.

'There's one, a street call office that is open all night — just before you get to

Bexley Heath,' he answered.

'Right,' said Blackmore. 'Then come on, Doctor, I want you to be kind enough to take charge of my secretary.'

He raced off to where he had left the car.

Harry had been laid on the back seat and covered with rugs, and the doctor and Frank Holland got in beside him, pulling down the emergency seats.

The detective jumped into the driving seat with Peekers beside him and as he pressed the self-starter and sent the great car once more roaring through the night his lips moved in a silent prayer that he would find Zatouroff before it was too late.

12

The Secret of the Purple Plague!

Blackmore saw the call box that the doctor had described standing under a lamp on an island in the centre of four cross roads, and pulled up.

A moment later he was rapidly turning the pages of the directory, searching for the private address of Ezra Marlow, and fervently hoping that that gentleman was on the telephone.

He found it at last with a little sigh of thankfulness, and gave the number. While he waited for a reply his fingers drummed impatiently on the glass wall of the little cabin. After what seemed an eternity a sleepy voice over the wire demanded:

'Who's there?'

As briefly as possible Blackmore explained what he wanted.

'Yes, I remember the transaction perfectly,' said the sleepy voice. 'I remember it perfectly because Leroy paid the money in notes, which is unusual. The name of the house you want is 'The Chase' and it stands in Angerston Road, Richmond. I should like to know — '

What Mr. Marlow would like to know Blackmore did not wait to find out. He banged the receiver on its hook and ran back to the car.

As he climbed once more to his place behind the wheel he looked at the illuminated clock on the dashboard, and set his teeth. Two hours only remained to get to Richmond, find Zatouroff and secure the antidote. Could he do it?

The car shot forward like a greyhound released from its trap as Blackmore's foot pressed down the accelerator, and if they had travelled fast on the journey down they positively flew on that race for life back.

The wind howled and shrieked about their ears and the car rocked and swayed from side to side as the detective coaxed every ounce of speed he could get from the powerful engine.

Once they nearly met with disaster, for

suddenly, and without warning a heavy lorry appeared from a side turning. Inspector Peekers caught his breath with a gasp. He knew that at the speed they were travelling it was impossible for Blackmore to pull up in time to avoid smashing into it, but with a twist of the wheel Blackmore sent the grey car across to the opposite side of the road, and with barely half an inch to spare they roared past the front of the lorry and on.

In an incredibly short space of time, although to the detective's strained nerves and anxiety torn mind the journey seemed endless, they reached London, and Blackmore was thankful that at that hour of the night there was little or no traffic about to heed their progress.

On the outskirts of Richmond the detective halted for a moment to enquire from a policeman on point duty the way to Angerston Road, and as he started off again, following the man's instructions, he looked again at the clock.

Only three quarters of an hour now remained!

In spite of the terrific speed they had

kept up he had been unable to do the journey from Dartford under the hour and a quarter.

Angerston Road proved to be a broad, short thoroughfare, lined on either side with an avenue of trees.

Blackmore brought the great car to a standstill at the beginning of the road and got out, switching off the lights as he did so.

'We don't want to give Zatouroff any inkling of our presence,' he said as Inspector Peekers and Frank Holland prepared to follow him. 'Our only chance is to take them by surprise. Look after my secretary, Doctor; I will get back as soon as possible.'

He set off briskly up the road in search of 'The Chase'. Presently, about half way along on the left hand side he came upon it. The name was painted in dirty white letters on the drive gates.

Blackmore stopped and surveyed the dark winding drive for a moment. Faintly visible behind a belt of trees was the shadowy outline of a house. It looked grim and deserted and not a light showed anywhere. Blackmore wondered for a moment if he had been mistaken, and his heart missed a beat as the doubt crept into his mind.

There was always the possibility that Zatouroff had not come here after all. If he had made a mistake it was too late now to rectify it, and Cartwright's life would pay the penalty.

The very idea sent a cold shudder through the detective, and for a moment he experienced a feeling of weakness, so that he had to steady himself by holding on to the gatepost for support.

He gritted his teeth, however, and fought the feeling down.

'Are you armed?' he whispered to Peekers, and the Inspector nodded. 'Follow me then,' said Blackmore, and the three of them proceeded swiftly and noiselessly in the direction of the house, keeping on a strip of grass that bordered the drive and deadened all sound of their footsteps.

It was a long, low, rambling structure of grey stone. The front windows of the ground floor were heavily shuttered and on one was a tattered bill still proclaiming the place for sale.

Blackmore saw at a glance that it would be impossible to gain an entrance in the front, and, followed by his companions, made his way towards a narrow path that turned off from the main drive and apparently led to the back. Here also the place was in complete darkness, but after making a quick survey the detective found what he was looking for — a small window set about three feet from the ground. He crept up to it and gently tried to raise the sash, but the hasp had evidently been slipped home, and it would not budge an inch.

He slipped his hand into his pocket and withdrew a penknife. Opening a large blade and with the assistance of Inspector Peekers he hoisted himself on to the broad ledge. Inserting the blade of the knife between the two sashes, he pressed. With a slight click the catch shot back, and the next second Blackmore had the window open.

He slipped into the room beyond and turned to assist Inspector Peekers and

Frank Holland through the window. Blackmore took an electric torch from his pocket, and as its rays cut through the darkness he saw that they were in a small empty room, which had at some time probably been a butler's pantry.

The door was ajar, and tiptoeing across to it John switched out the light of his torch and stood listening intently. His heart gave a bound as he heard from somewhere close at hand the muffled murmur of voices. Stepping cautiously through the door he tried to locate the direction from which the sound came.

He was in a passage, and the voices appeared to be proceeding from a door several yards on his right. John crept towards it, followed by Inspector Peekers and Holland. As he drew near it he saw a faint gleam of light It was only a single starlike speck and Blackmore guessed that it was shining through a keyhole. Blackmore bent down and applied his eyes to the aperture.

The room was evidently a large kitchen and was empty, save for a big deal table and a few chairs that occupied the centre of the room. Seated at the table talking to three other men, amongst whom Blackmore recognized Bertram Albrey, was Zatouroff!

The table was piled with what appeared to be printed handbills, and by the side of these were stacks of white envelopes.

Zatouroff was speaking and now that he was close to the door Blackmore could hear distinctly what he was saying.

'The sooner we put the scheme into operation, and clear out of the country the better,' came the doctor's rasping voice. 'Now we know that that confounded meddler, John Blackmore, is poking his nose into our affairs, we can't afford to waste time. I propose therefore that we start the operations tomorrow.'

There was a murmur of assent from the others.

'In order that there can be no mistake,' continued Zatouroff, 'I had better repeat the whole details to you.'

He reached across the table and drew towards him several sheets of foolscap.

'Here is a list of all the wealthiest men at the present moment in London. It includes several well-known millionaires, American. To each one of them that I have marked one of these pamphlets will be sent, enclosed in one of our special oilskin, airtight envelopes.' He paused and chuckled. 'Each envelope will be marked 'Personal' so that on no account will there be a possibility of its being opened by anyone excepting the person to whom it is addressed. The pamphlet it contains, will, of course, prior to its being sealed in the envelope, be impregnated with the germs of the 'Purple Plague'. The moment any one of these people handle that pamphlet they will become inoculated with the disease, and unless they comply with the demand which is printed thereon they will die within twenty-four hours. As I say, they are all wealthy men and they will be only too glad to hand over to our messenger the substantial sums of money we demand. The moment the money is received by us — and I have stipulated that it shall be paid in treasury notes which cannot be traced — each one will receive, by telephone, a prescription for the antidote to the Plague.'

'Suppose they have our messenger arrested,' said Bertram.

'They won't,' declared Zatouroff. 'For they know that the result will mean their own death. The newspapers have already helped us considerably by giving so much publicity to the previous deaths that occurred as a result of my experiments. No. I have worked the whole scheme out in detail, as you know, and I can't see any possibility of failure. By this time the day after tomorrow — ' he raised his voice triumphantly — 'we should, between us, be in the possession of a huge fortune, which I have roughly calculated to be in the region of five million pounds!'

Blackmore listened horror-stricken as he heard the cool way in which Zatouroff detailed the most ghastly plot that had ever been devised by a human brain! So this was the secret of the 'Purple Plague'! Blackmail on a gigantic scale!

John Blackmore shuddered as he realized how near Doctor Zatouroff had been to getting away with his scheme, and a wave of fury swept over him against the man who could have conceived such a diabolical idea.

He straightened up, and placing his lips close to Inspector Peekers' ear he whispered:

'Zatouroff and the rest are in here. Get your revolver ready and we'll take them by surprise.'

Blackmore gently tried the handle of the door and discovered that it was unlocked and then drawing his own weapon he suddenly flung it open and stepped into the room.

'The game's up, Doctor Zatouroff,' he said grimly, covering the doctor with his revolver.

There was an exclamation of alarm and surprise from the men at the table.

'Good Heavens! Blackmore!' gasped Bertram Albrey.

'Put your hands up, all of you, and don't move,' snapped Blackmore.

'Now, Zatouroff,' he continued, turning to the doctor, 'I'll give you until I count three to hand over the antidote to the 'Purple Plague' otherwise I'll put a bullet through your brain!'

13

Conclusion

Doctor Zatouroff looked at John Blackmore steadily, and his eyes narrowed until they appeared mere slits in the parchment face.

Inspector Peekers had slipped to the detective's side and was covering Bertram and the other two.

'One,' began Blackmore crisply. 'Two — '

Before he could count three Zatouroff suddenly ducked, grasped the big table and heaved it up towards Blackmore.

It was done in an instant. The detective fired twice, but at the same moment a corner of the table caught him on the wrist and knocked the pistol from his hand, and sent him staggering into Inspector Peekers.

One of Blackmore's bullets found a billet, however, for with a gasping cry Bertram Albrey clapped his hand to his side and collapsed on to the floor. The other two men sprang upon the Inspector before he could recover his balance and bore him to the ground.

Doctor Zatouroff had drawn a revolver from his pocket when Blackmore leaped across the overturned table and gripping his wrists wrested the weapon from his grasp.

With a snarl of rage Zatouroff closed with him and they fell to the floor with a crash. Blackmore was uppermost, and before the doctor could throw him off he had seized his arm, and, jerking himself back, dragged Zatouroff's left arm with him. Twisting his right leg across the doctor's throat he held him helpless in that terrible ju-jitsu grip, the arm lock, which is used after a fall.

Zatouroff soon proved that he was no novice in the art of ju-jitsu and he fought like a tiger to use the counter to that hold, but Blackmore tightened the pressure on Zatouroff's neck and dragged the doctor's left arm still further over his inner thigh. Another inch and the bone would snap. A smothered groan of agony burst from the doctor's lips.

The pistol that Blackmore had twisted from his grasp was lying near and still keeping his grip on Zatouroff with one hand, the detective reached out his other arm and picked it up.

'Now,' panted Blackmore, pressing the barrel to the doctor's forehead, 'the antidote — quick or by heavens I'll shoot you with as little compunction as I would a mad dog!'

'In the cupboard,' gasped Zatouroff. 'Bottle — with — red label.'

'How is it used — quick!' grated Blackmore.

'Hypodermically,' said the doctor. 'There's a — syringe — there — to — once full — ' Still keeping Zatouroff covered with the pistol, Blackmore looked round to see what had happened to Peekers.

Frank Holland had gone to the Inspector's assistance and between them they had managed to overpower the other men. One was unconscious from the effects of a blow which the young man had delivered with the butt of the

Inspector's heavy automatic and Peekers was just rising to his feet, having handcuffed the other.

'Here,' snapped Blackmore, 'come and look after this scoundrel while I attend to Cartwright.'

He handed his pistol to the Inspector and releasing his hold on Zatouroff rose to his feet.

'See if you can find some rope, and bind him securely,' he said as he hurried to the cupboard in the corner.

There were several bottles with red labels and beside them a leather case containing a hypodermic syringe.

John only waited to make sure and then he ran out of the kitchen and down the passage to the back door. Unbolting it he raced round to the main drive and down the street to the place where he had left the car.

'I've got the antidote,' he jerked, in answer to the doctor's question as he sent the car forward with a bound and turned in at the drive gate. 'I only pray to Heaven I've got it in time!'

At the little pathway leading round to

the back he stopped, and lifting Harry gently carried him into the kitchen, followed by the doctor.

Inspector Peekers and. Holland had cut down the sash lines from the windows and with these had securely bound Zatouroff and his two companions.

Bertram Albrey had passed beyond reach of earthly punishment, for Blackmore's deflected bullet had pierced his heart and the man was dead.

Peekers and the young man hurried to the detective's assistance, righted the overturned table, and on this Harry was laid.

The secretary was no longer breathing stertorously and over his set face a faint bluish tinge was creeping. The doctor bent over him and made a swift examination, shaking his head.

'I'm afraid we are too late, Mr. Blackmore,' he said.

The detective felt his eyes grow moist as he gazed at the still, silent form of his secretary.

'We can but try,' he answered huskily.

He brought one of the bottles from the

cupboard and swiftly fitted the syringe together while the doctor unfastened Cartwright's cuff and bared the forearm.

Blackmore bent forward, and having filled the syringe from the bottle inserted the needle-sharp point beneath Harry's skin and pressed home the plunger.

A minute passed. Two . . . three . . . and then to the expectant group round the table, and to John Blackmore in particular, each one seemed an age.

But nothing happened. Harry remained still and silent, not even the slightest sign of breathing disturbing that rigid body.

And then, at the expiration of twenty minutes — the longest Blackmore had ever known in his life — a faint tinge of colour began to creep slowly into the young man's face and presently an almost imperceptible sigh escaped his parted lips.

The doctor leaned forward and peered closely at the secretary.

'The antidote has taken effect,' he said. 'The danger is past. He will live!'

And John Blackmore uttered a prayer of thankfulness for the saving of the young man who was as much to him as if he had been his own brother.

* * *

It was several days before Cartwright was able to leave his bed, and over a fortnight before he had totally recovered and was back again to his normal self.

Edna Lister had been found bound and gagged in an upper room in the house at Richmond, and beyond the shock resulting from her experience was unharmed.

John Blackmore, who had long suspected that Doctor Zatouroff was in reality the man who had married James Albrey's sister and deserted her, had his suspicion confirmed beyond any doubt by an examination of the doctor's private papers at his flat in Wyman Chambers. His real name, it being discovered, was Julian Ansell.

The trial of Doctor Zatouroff and his two confederates, Mason and Mitchell, some two months later, and the exposure of their ghastly plot in connection with the 'Purple Plague' created a sensation, and the newspapers had to publish special editions to satisfy an eager public who clamoured for the latest reports.

It was on John Blackmore's evidence, principally, that Zatouroff was found guilty and sentenced to death for his many crimes. Mason and Mitchell each received a sentence of penal servitude for life as accessories.

In deference to Edna Lister's feelings and to prevent the girl being branded as the daughter of a murderer, Blackmore, with the assistance of Edward Cranston, succeeded in suppressing the truth regarding the girl's parentage, and to this day, Edna Lister, who was brought up from her birth by the worthy couple who had looked after her mother in her last illness, believed them to be her real parents and is ignorant of the truth.

It was a month after the sentence passed on Doctor Zatouroff, or, to give him his real name, Ansell, had been executed and the civilised world rid of a fiendish and inhuman monster, that John Blackmore and Cartwright, taking advantage of a slack day and an unusually fine afternoon, were strolling in the Park.

As they walked slowly and leisurely along by the Row a girl and a young man, mounted on two superb horses, cantered past. Blackmore raised his hat and the girl smiled and bowed.

'Who was that, sir?' asked Harry, who had been looking in the opposite direction and had turned just in time to witness the action.

'That,' said John, 'was Edna Lister — or — to be exact, Mrs. Frank Holland!'

And with a reminiscent look in his eyes John Blackmore gazed after the disappearing riders.

THE END

We do hope that you have enjoyed reading this large print book.

Did you know that all of our titles are available for purchase?

We publish a wide range of high quality large print books including:
Romances, Mysteries, Classics
General Fiction
Non Fiction and Westerns

Special interest titles available in large print are:
The Little Oxford Dictionary
Music Book, Song Book
Hymn Book, Service Book

Also available from us courtesy of Oxford University Press:
Young Readers' Dictionary
(large print edition)
Young Readers' Thesaurus
(large print edition)

For further information or a free brochure, please contact us at:
Ulverscroft Large Print Books Ltd.,
The Green, Bradgate Road, Anstey,
Leicester, LE7 7FU, England.
Tel: (00 44) 0116 236 4325
Fax: (00 44) 0116 234 0205

Other titles in the
Linford Mystery Library:

DEADLY MEMOIR

Ardath Mayhar

When Margaret Thackrey, ex-government agent and writer, decides to pen her memoirs, she unwittingly gets the attention of a vicious assassin — a man whose nefarious deeds she'd nearly uncovered during her service. Now he must stop the publication of her book before his true character is revealed. He murders Margaret's husband, and stalks her from Oregon to Texas, where she must finally confront her past — and a determined, stone-cold killer!

THE GRAB

Gordon Landsborough

In Istanbul, a beautiful girl is grabbed from her hotel bed and taken out into the night. But Professional Trouble-Buster Joe P. Heggy is looking on and decides to investigate: who was the girl and why was she kidnapped? But when thugs try to eliminate him, he is equal to their attempts, especially when he's aided by a bunch of American construction workers. Then things get very tense when Heggy finds the girl — and then kidnaps her himself . . .